Henry Breneton Marriott Watson

The Heart of Miranda

And Other Stories, Being Mostly Winter Tales

Henry Breneton Marriott Watson

The Heart of Miranda
And Other Stories, Being Mostly Winter Tales

ISBN/EAN: 9783337007676

Printed in Europe, USA, Canada, Australia, Japan

Cover: Foto ©Andreas Hilbeck / pixelio.de

More available books at **www.hansebooks.com**

The Heart of Miranda

The Heart of Miranda

And other Stories, being mostly

Winter Tales

BY

H. B. MARRIOTT WATSON

JOHN LANE: THE BODLEY HEAD

LONDON AND NEW YORK

1898

TO HENRY JAMES

Dear Henry James:

If the appearance of this brief dedication would seem to lay upon you the onerous obligation of reading the pages that follow, pray let me make it clear that I look for no such magnanimous return. I beg that you will rather understand that here is the tribute of one who holds your work in such consideration that, having nothing else to offer save his admiration, he takes leave to set it forth in this public fashion, even if only as a prelude to his own disjected pieces.

Yours always sincerely,

H. B. Marriott Watson.

Chiswick, March 21, 1898.

Contents

The Heart of Miranda

I. THE POPINJAY

Miranda came forth into the garden and looked about her. The sun shone through deeps of blue, the spring flowers were blowing, the young breezes of the morning fluttered her bright hair. Her white gown trembled and wavered. In her large eyes the light gleamed as on the surface of deep pools. Merrily sang the birds as they flitted among the trees. Her gaze wandered abroad, from the garden, fresh with its early dews, to the rolling hills and distant valleys, shrouded in the golden haze of the morning. She smiled at the landscape. Something knocked at Miranda's heart.

The Heart of Miranda

Miranda felt the world was full of charm; it held something in keeping for her, something unknown and wonderful and fair. Of what does a young maid dream in the fresh morning? Soft and blooming from her sleep, she surveyed the world and its bountiful contents. All things lovely came to lie at Miranda's feet. She could have danced for gaiety ; she could have sung for happiness. What enchanting avenues of pleasure opened out before her eyes! Something was waiting for her; she wondered what. Its nature and its quality evaded her; but she had a vague vision of a great glory near by, ready for her discovery. Her pulse beat fast. Something mysterious was creeping into her heart. She was but a child in years. How could she know? Within the phantasmagoria of her dreams she wandered in innocence. The air that breathed about her forehead she smiled at for pleasure; the sun that shone so warmly on her cheeks she laughed at for sheer delight; the flowers that nodded on their stalks she kissed for very happiness. Youth, spring, and loveliness blossomed in Miranda's heart.

Miranda looked down the pathway and wondered. She could not rest within doors. The mystery in her heart turned her steps away into the garden and the world, to seek, to seek—she wondered what. Her soul went out among the flowers and rejoiced, and then crept back and nestled in its home, marvelling. She yearned for something other than the flowers and the sunshine, something in harmony with them. Would she find it at the end of the pathway, or in the wide world? She tripped down the steps and set forth.

At the corner of the garden, where the stile led into the lane, Miranda paused. A pretty youth peeped over the hedge and gazed upon her. Before the admiration in his glance Miranda's eyes fell. She fingered the daffodils at her breast until he should be gone, but when she looked up again he was still there. Miranda stamped her little foot.

"When you have stared your fill, Sir," said she, "perhaps I shall have leave to pass."

He plucked off his hat and asked her pardon, and his hair hung in curls.

"You shall have all the liberty I can give you, fair maid," said he, "if I, too, may pass with you."

"But why?" asked Miranda, smoothing her flowers, with downcast eyes.

He smiled a pretty smile. "Oh," says he, "but you know you are beautiful. The pretty must always have full knowledge of their own prettiness." And he preened his bare head with an elegant white hand and smiled to himself.

Miranda looked up. He was quite the

most ravishing creature she had seen. She wondered. Miranda looked down, and the scent of the garden passed into her soul. He put out his hand to help her over the stile, but she kept her eyelids lowered.

" Will you not trust me ? " he lisped. She shook her head, and mounted the first stage.

" Of what age ? " he asked sweetly. She climbed the steps one by one.

" Eighteen," she answered shyly.

"Jump," he cried, " and I will catch you."

He opened his arms; she looked and hesitated. She put her face aside and crept down the steps demurely.

" Cruel!" he murmured, using his soft eyes upon her. He sighed and turned away. Miranda surveyed the valley mistily.

" 'Tis a sweet age for a maid," said he at length.

Miranda laughed. She clapped her hands in the glory of the springtide.

" And mine own can match it," he went on. " Betwixt yours and mine are but a summer or two."

" 'Tis a fine age for a man," says Miranda, slyly.

He turned swiftly and took her hand. Miranda's heart stopped dead.

" Think you so, sweet ?" he asked softly. " I have long looked for such a maid as you. We should make a pretty pair."

Miranda's heart beat slowly.

" What does it mean ?" said Miranda.

" It means," said he, " my sweet, that the world is ours before us, that time and space are browbeat out of reckoning, that life is love and love is life, my darling."

" What is love ?" asked Miranda.

" Look in my face," he said, " and, faith, sweetheart, you shall see it there. It is engraven on my heart for you; it is imprinted in my eyes. Every negotiation of this body is but for you. Come, let me gaze into your soul, and see what you have sight of in this soul of mine."

" I see it not," said Miranda.

He seized her fingers. " Let me kiss your hand," said he.

" No, no!" said Miranda.

" Your lips!" he cried.

" Hush! hush!" said Miranda.

Her face blew red; she snatched her hand away, and turned aside. With a light step, he followed after, pleading in her ears.

" You love me, dear; I know you love me," he whispered. " It is but your innocence that keeps you from the knowledge. Have I not seen the light in other eyes, and shall I not judge? Faith, dear, hundreds have pined for these blue eyes of mine."

Miranda's heart went to and fro about its business.

" You are mistaken," said she, sedately; " the light in my eyes, if so there be a light, is the dancing of the sun. As for this love,

I know it not. And you," she cried, looking upon him with a little scorn, "whatever you may see in your own, as you bow and caper before your mirror, pray pause and question if it be not merely the reflection of a very precious vanity, the admiration of your own fine person. You are a pretty fellow," says she, surveying him.

He smirked and bowed.

"I vowed you would see it soon," said he, complacently.

"But for my own taste," quoth Miranda, cocking her head upon one side, "you smack overmuch of the toilet-table. You are composed too daintily as a waxen image; you are prepared too fragrantly as with my lady's powder. You are too tricked with all the fashions at your service."

"Madame," says he in astonishment, "your tongue is awry to-day. It is some bitterness, surely, makes you so reckless of your words."

"Nay," said Miranda, soberly; "but I am cool enough. I but survey you as you are in all your maiden vanity. You offer me love, and what do I that know not the foolish term make out this love to be? Why, forsooth, yourself is all it comes to; yourself, or as much as goes to make yourself, of all the tricks and elegances of the hour. I would take no love at such an estimate. It comes with the hour, and with the hour it goes. Sir, 'tis not worth the time of a ' pish ' or a ' tush.' "

"You have a vile temper," he rejoined, crossly; " I have never met a maid with such a shrewish wit as yours—no, not among the thousands that have loved me. What have I done to offend you? But I know the way of a maid's tongue," he said, wagging his head; " if she be crossed even by the slipping of an epithet, she will straightway fall into a very tempest of rage and deny the dearest idol of her heart. Lord, how perverse she will be! Come, sweet my love, and tell me how I have offended, for it is not in reason but you must love me."

" Love you!" cried Miranda, and laughed to the sky. She looked him up and down. " I like not your nose," quoth she, " 'tis too straight for my taste—'tis wonderful how monotonous a nose may be. And your eyes," she exclaimed, " Heavens! of what pale China blue, as the eyes of an idol grinning on his thousand worshippers! There is less colour in a kind of blue I know than in any honest puddle of mud. And, oh! my pretty sir, to find the petulance of a maid pouting on the lips of a youth! 'Tis so unseemly. Those curling locks, too, I cannot abide. On my soul, they are more ladylike and bewitching than mine own, and no woman would forgive such an affront upon her vanity. Love you, sweet sir! I love not a mannikin, designed by Mother Nature as fit company for the lapdog on my lady's knee. Give me a man," says Miranda, blazing into anger; " give me a man with a soul and body fashioned for manhood."

He stamped his foot, and made as though to seize her by the wrist, but stopped.

" Pooh!" he sneered, as he turned away; " 'tis a comfort fair women fade so fast."

II. THE BELLS OF FOLLY

Miranda ran into the meadow laughing. The grassy slope shelved down into the valley, where the wood lay black and still. Daffodils nodded and cowslips bowed as she passed upon her way. A lark got up and rose singing to heaven. She sped out of the shadow and into the sunlight, and the sound of her young laughter floated down the valley; echoes joined it there, and the little ravine gurgled with merriment. Miranda stopped, with her chin in the air, and listened. Was it all the echo of her own delight, or was it something more ? The peal of her mockery died into the sombre copse, and out of it, fresh and clear, a voice trilled merrily on its upward way. Miranda stood and waited.

He came up the bank of wild flowers, his face bright with the love of life and laughter, and at the sight of her he paused. The two faced each other for a while in silence, and then a smile ran round Miranda's lips, and the young man's eyes sparkled with merriment.

" I took your laughter for a signal," said he, making his beaming salutations; " but I reckoned little upon so charming an assignation."

" It was but a signal of the spring, Sir," says she, with a dainty bow.

" Nay," he replied; " I make no such distinctions between the seasons. I laugh the whole year through; it is the manner of the wise. You will perceive my jocund humour, fair mistress. Believe me, 'tis not the whim of an hour contrived by the guiles of a spring morning; but a very settled disposition of the mind. I am broad-based upon gaiety."

"Ah! to be gay!" cried Miranda; "to be gay is to live."

"Life is at our feet," said the merry youth. "I take an infinite pleasure in its complexities. Believe me, nothing should matter, save the twinkling of an eye or the dimpling of a cheek."

"You are right," said Miranda, smiling. "How can one have enough of laughter?"

"We are of one mind," he answered pleasantly. "Let us go into our corner and be merry together."

"Why not?" says Miranda. "Why not?"

": There are ten thousand pleasures in this silly world," he went on; "and, for myself,

I have not yet exhausted the tenth part of them. Count my years, then, and make three-score-and-ten the dividend, and what remains? Pack them into the hours never so neatly, and you will not exhaust the store. And that is why I am a spendthrift of pleasures. I eke not out my delights. I would burn twenty in a straw hat out of sheer caprice, and toss a dozen to the ducks upon the lake for pity.''

'' Yes, yes,'' agreed Miranda.

'' Time—'' he continued, with fine scorn. '' Time has discovered us a conspiracy of the ages to enthrone this Melancholy. But we are no traitors to our rightful king, you and I ; and we will clap a crown upon the head of Laughter, and lay the usurper by the heels in his proper dungeon.''

'' He were better there,'' replied Miranda, thoughtfully.

'' There is never a care,'' he resumed, '' upon which we may not trample, not a trouble which we may not forget. What a fool is he who would nurse his sorrow and not bury it in the deepest grave!"

"What a fool!" murmured Miranda, dreamily.

"Should one lose a friend, a fig for friendship!" quoth he. "Does one cast a lover, a snap for a hundred lovers! What has been remains, and what is shall be."

Miranda said nothing.

"Subtract love from life," said the young man, "and life remains. I would have the world know that love is a pleasant cipher, an amiable and entertaining mood, and that life is left when love is lost. There is no Love. It were more truly writ in the plural and spelled with a small letter."

Miranda turned upon him swiftly. "Fie! fie!" said she, and the light flashed in her eyes. "I know nothing of this Love, but I dare swear there be things that matter. Take these from life, and what will rest

over? Is there not Sorrow, and is there not
Pain? Is there not Remorse, and is there
not the thing called Sin? I know nothing of
these; I am too young to the world. But
there they stand, Sir, importuning at our
doors with outstretched arms, and one has
only to lift the latch to let them in. You
would deny the very pulse of human nature
when you ignore these evils. You would
forswear the very weaknesses which have
composed for you your sentiments."

In the excitement of her retort Miranda's
face flushed and grew bright. Wide-eyed,
the young man stared at her and forgot to
laugh, and when she had done his head
dropped and he sighed.

"Ah," she said, "you sigh. You yourself have felt and suffered. You have be-
lied yourself! You sigh. There are facts
in life even for sighs."

"'Tis true," he answered softly, "yet I
sighed for pleasure."

"What pleasure?" she asked curiously.

"Or it may be hope," he added.

He looked at her, and his gaze was mild and wistful. She regarded him in perplexity, and then a wild flush took her in the cheek and throat.

"Pooh! pooh!" she cried, and turned off, plucking at the hawthorn bush. The white may smelled rank, but strange and soothing; the petals shivered and fell. Miranda's heart beat on, wondering. Something clapped at its doors again and again. Would she open? What was this impatient visitor that pleaded so for entrance? She had so little knowledge; she was but newly arrived upon the world. Her emotions were still strangers to her; she was a pilgrim still among her new sensations. Ought she to open? Nay, to stay so and wonder was surely pleasantest. One day she would throw wide the doors and look. But now it was sweet to feel that hand upon the knocker, that clutching at the latch, and lie trembling within in feigned insecurity. She turned and faced him. Straightway the clamour ceased, and in her heart was silence. She looked him coldly in the face.

"You smile for love?" she asked.

"Yes, dear," said he, "and for the thought of you."

"Oh, you take me too lightly," she broke out. "You do not guess what a solemn thing this Love may be. You flutter into a thousand follies on the scantest reflection. You will dance, and you will play, and you will jingle-jangle through your holiday world without a thought for anything but pirouettes and jigs and whirligigs of laughter. The most sonorous of sacred sorrows may sound in your ears, and wake no echo but a jape within your heart. And you would put me upon that dead plane of ribald merriment with yourself? I will laugh with you. Yes; I will go beg of you for jests in my jocund seasons. I am willing to shriek over your whimsicalities at my own pleasure. In my serene, unthinking moments I will be content to exchange humours with you, and to vow life were void and dull were not such as you at my beck. But when I have opened my chamber and fastened the door upon myself my soul and I shall be alone together; and I will weep, and pity, and repent, and ache out my heart with sorrow in which you can have no lot. I am young, but I have an inkling of what the world may mean."

"The world," said he, "means happiness."

"The world," she retorted, "means tears, and bitter wringing of the hands. Have I not heard of Death? And have I not seen Pain? You think me gay, yet how long shall I keep this gaiety in my heart? I go round upon the wheel. It turns and changes. What shall befall to-morrow that

I should not weep to-day? You would pluck me with no greater consideration than you would pick a flower from its stalk wherewith to deck your coat. Should it wither or fall adust, another will serve until the coming of the wine. Look you, you will sigh and weep for love, and your sighs will be smiles, and your tears will be laughter. Forthright your heart is singing like a lark. Yours! yours is the shallowest of paltry passions.''

" I would do much for you," said he.

" Give up your dimples," cried Miranda, " and so to the churchyard with a wry face."

" Even that," he answered, nodding.

" Pah!" said she, " you will not contain your face lugubriously for five minutes by the clock. Though you shall remember to be sober for two sentences, at the third you will be whistling, and the fourth will find you holding your sides."

He moved a step towards her.

" And if I should die for you?" he asked pleadingly.

Miranda gasped. She contemplated his face with uncertainty. His eyes shone with the dew of tears; his hands trembled; it was the corner of his mouth betrayed him. Miranda burst into laughter.

" You!" she cried. " You! Why, you would forget my coffin as it passed, and the colour of my face ere my back was upon you. See here," she said; " I will give you to the hedge for misery; but I swear you will take the lane as jauntily as an hour since. Get you gone, my merry man, and come again to dispute with me in an idle humour. Fie! fie! to think on you and Death in the same company!"

He sighed and turned away.

" You have the smallest heart of any maid I know," he said, shaking his head.

" The better for my laughter," laughed Miranda.

He moved across the meadow, his head hanging, his eyes downcast, his stick dragging among the daisies. Miranda stared after him, her lips parted in amusement. He climbed the stile, and, stopping on the topmost step, turned to her again.

"I have at least one solace," he called across the meadow. "I shall forget your fickle face by night."

Miranda's laughter touched the skies and ceased. Her face fell thoughtful; she sighed and shrugged her dainty shoulders.

III. THE PHILOSOPHY OF LOVE

"Is there such a thing as Love?" asked Miranda.

Overhead the larks sung, about her the blackbirds carolled; finch called to finch in the hedgerows. Wrinkled with her thoughts, Miranda walked down the slope into the field of young green corn, and, pausing on the verge of the wheat, looked across the valley.

"Is there such a thing as Love?" she asked.

She shaded her eyes to the East. The morning still lay like a golden shroud upon the horizon, and through that veil she could not pierce. She wondered what reached beyond that remote, mysterious brightness. If the sun would but disperse those aureoles of the East, she would, perhaps, see clearly what she guessed at vaguely. The valley was her own, informed and animated by her own fancy, free to her wandering feet, charged full of sweet beatitudes, smiling with flowers, and lovely with the serene possession of life and happiness. But Miranda had, somehow, a dim sense of confinement within those golden mists. Her life was beautiful and fortunate, but the walls of the world came so close upon her. She wanted the key of the wicket to pass out upon the mountains. Was there nothing beyond the birds and the flowers and the waving fields of wheat? Something troubled Miranda!

There was none to guide her. What passed beyond the mists and what fell across the mountains? She was sure she should know some day, but she wanted to know now. So many mysteries flitted through Miranda's mind.

"If there is no Love," said Miranda, "what is ringing at my heart? Is it Love, is it Death, or is it merely the desire and delight of life? Oh, for an interpreter!" she sighed.

In the little pathway through the corn a bird lay dead. Miranda stooped and smoothed its ruffled feathers.

"Is it Pity?" she asked. "Perhaps it is Pity," she said.

She could not dissever her emotions; they

ran together in confusion. The one faded into the other. How fast the blood fled through Miranda's body! How full was Miranda's soul!

"He must be very tender," thought Miranda, stroking the poor dead creature. "He must be very kind and true. How shall I know him? What does it mean?"

The wind sang through the wheat, and seemed to bear snatches from over the mountains to her ears. They stirred her strangely. She threw her arms up in despair.

"Oh, I shall never love!" sighed Miranda, "for love is all a figment."

"So young a maid, and yet so harsh a creed," said a voice behind her.

Miranda started, and hung her head for shame.

"If I have trespassed upon your thoughts," said the voice, "it was through the inadvertence of an impulse. Forgive me. I should have passed and left you to your trouble."

" I am in no trouble," said Miranda, glancing shyly at the stranger. " I was but wondering."

" The most of our life is wonder, and the rest regret," said he.

" Mine is all wonder, Sir," she answered.

He nodded his head kindly.

" Yes," he sighed. " The garden still encloses you. You are not yet upon the road. And the garden is full of flowers, and the road winds through hot and arid tracts to death."

Miranda looked at him timidly, and he was watching the valley with a gentle smile. Hope. danced through Miranda's heart. Was this then her interpreter, who would put a meaning upon her unknown wonders and solve the mysteries that beset her?

" Yet those in the garden may dream of

the road," she said; "and I am perplexed with many things."

"This Love," he answered, smiling, "most of all."

Miranda blushed. "'Tis true," she murmured.

"Love, poor child," said the stranger, "is a tyrannous enemy, but a decent friend. It were better in chains than above an altar."

"Is it not good?" she asked in surprise.

He leaned upon the gate. "It is easily mistook," he said slowly. "Who am I to convince you? But my years in the world have taught me to regard it at the best as a very tender tie of friendship."

"But, oh!" says Miranda.

"Child," said he, "you will cry your heart out for it, and once it is gained will cry out your heart because of it. Believe me, Love is a steady flame, and neither leaps nor splutters."

"How may one tell it?" whispered Miranda.

"Shall one say by the voice?" he answered. "Shall one speak of the touch, or the look? Maybe, a little breathlessness will mark it."

"I have that now," says she.

"Well, well," he replied; "but 'tis of a long growth and very gentle."

"And may not one love at sight?" asked Miranda.

He laughed. "My child, 'twould be the veriest folly and bitterly repented. Never yet came true love but by slow years of wont. A face—a face is a shadow that passes. Eyes—eyes flicker and fade. Lips —lips are for food and laughter. The hair decays; the body dwindles and withers; the comely limbs grow shrunken and hollow. If you would hold by these, my dear, you would put your trust in the flying hour."

Miranda's eyes opened large and wide.

She stared at him. Her underlip quivered. She gave a little sob, and at the sound he turned to her. For the first time her face came full into the sunlight, and her eyes met his. He took her hand; she hid her face.

" Why, child——" said he.

" Is it so?" she whispered, " and is it really so? Will all this come to me?"

He looked in her eyes again, and drew a sharp breath.

" Dear," he answered, " it is the way of mortal clay."

Miranda sighed.

" But, ah!" he cried, " surely the gods will spare such sweetness till the end."

He held her hand still. She wondered.

" And must one wait so long?" she asked.

He shook his head. " I believe," said he, fiercely, " that upon occasion Love may come at sight."

" Why," said she, opening her eyes in wonder, " a little ago it was the veriest folly!"

" Ah, dear," he answered, " forgive me. I was blind, and saw not. Philosophy and I rolled into the ditch." Miranda stared at him. He smiled and sighed. " But when it comes," said he, " it comes indeed. The skies open, the flowers blow sweetly, every shred of green corn is fragrant. Love, believe me, is a very comfortable possession."

" Is it not gentle?" asked Miranda.

" Ah, so gentle!" he replied. " It wraps you round like a soft fur; it soothes you; you may sit and dine and sleep with easy thoughts if Love but guard you. Love is like a good wine, that mellows the heart and quickens the understanding."

He moved a little closer to her.

" Were one to love like this," said Miranda, " would the heart be then at rest? Would it throb less loudly in one's side?

Would such a love fulfil the most exigent desires of human nature? What part would so smooth a sentiment fill in one's life?"

" Passion," he answered, " is the bubble that we blow in youth. It is the creature of our own imagination, fails with our pulse, and expires upon the indrawing of a breath. How many have I seen wrecked upon passion, incredulous that it would be gone with the fall of the sun or the waking of the birds! Love, child, is no passion, but the sweetest of contentments. Served in a daily fare, it will preserve Peace and Health and Wisdom. What would you have beyond these? For, behold! the greatest of all is Peace."

" Peace!" sighed Miranda.

He went towards her. "Ah, sweet," he murmured, " Peace should be our fortune should we go through life together. Come, place your hand in mine, and we will dispel these rebel wildings from your heart. Look round and see the spring. All things keep serene and quiet holiday. Pluck out distrust; forget these treacherous longings! A happy childhood shall surely preface a comfortable career of ease.''

Miranda hesitated; her pretty brows were puckered with doubt. At his bidding she looked around. Nature smiled at her. The face of the world shone with gaiety. Somewhere in the elms a throstle sang of Love and mystery. She turned and gazed into the stranger's face, and his kindly eyes seemed dull and old. Spring and the sunshine and the song of birds lay not therein. She shook her head.

'' I want not comfortable ease,'' she answered sadly; '' I would not take it at so great a sacrifice. See, there are other things in Nature save peace. What of this dead bird, callow from the nest? Is it nought but peace I hear in yonder singing in the trees? Hark! what secret is the young corn breathing to itself? Nay, what is even this poor ignorant heart of mine faltering within me? All around I see witnesses to some greater glory than this ease of which you speak. The strokes of my pulse beat folly, you will say. Well, I will pursue their folly until wisdom comes. Do not let me from my own. I can but follow where myself am leader.''

'' Nay,'' he said; '' follow rather where I lead—I who have years of wisdom. You are very sweet to me. Your eyes are soft and beautiful.''

'' Eyes flicker and fade,'' said Miranda with a smile.

'' Your form is young and lissom.''

''The body dwindles,'' quoth she, pouting.

'' Your lips——'' he began.

'' Are for food and laughter,'' laughed Miranda. '' I pray you will not hold by these, else will you put your trust in the flying hour.''

" You mock me," said he sadly.

" Nay," she replied; " I give you back the echo of your own philosophy. Is it not true ? Yourself have seen it. They shrink, they wither, they fade, they decay—oh, it were wanton vanity to admire them! Sir, you have a very wise head, and will do well not to go back upon its counsels. Nay, you shall have your comfort, and you shall take it at the lips of any of a hundred maids. There is no choice for you. Why, no mysteries may trouble you. You have but a straight course to saunter by, without so much as blinking at the sun. Marry your maid then, and take your comfort in God's name. And in my mind's eye I shall see you lolling in your purple chair, and sucking in the comfort of your admirable room, smoking your comfortable pipe, and directing comfortable glances at the flight of rooks outside your window. And beside you one, I shall see, to tender anticipations to your wants, plump and brown and gentle, the mother of your sturdy children and the custodian of your ease. Oh, you shall have a comfortable life, I do assure you.''

''That,'' he said tenderly, ''is how I would paint the picture for myself and— you. Come, think upon it. What better prospect than this home you have upheld to mockery? Indeed, what you have framed in derision shall surely come to be your heart's desire. Forego your yearnings: they are idle dreams. Why, then, dream them at night if you will, so be you are complacently mine by day. I exact not much, but a warm affection and a tender friendship.''

''Oh, we may be friends! we may be friends!'' cried Miranda. ''I will be a dozen friends to you a day. I love the friendliness of friends, as I love the light and warmth of the sun. I will dance with you, if you be not too staid; I will sing with you, if you have but the voice; I will read my books in tears with you, if you can weep. But then you shall march home to your comfortable wife, embrace her serenely, and, free from the distractions of your friend's emotions, serenely take comfort in her serene comfortableness."

" Ah!" he cried.

" But as for me," she went on, with an imperious gesture of her hand, " I like not comfort. I can buy a rushlight for a farthing, bread for a penny, and the whole world for sixpence. I would think shame to sell the mysteries of life for the petty possession of a bland prosperity."

Without a word, he turned on his heel and went his way, and Miranda, following him with her eyes, smiled to herself and her heart. She was flushed and beautiful; her bosom quickened with excitement, and to the door of her heart the hand came clutching, clutching at the latch.

IV. THE MAN OF SENTIMENT

A sound of hurrying feet struck on Miranda's ear. She turned in time to confront two eager eyes that were bent upon her brightly. He was a little breathless with his haste, and his smooth cheeks were flushed with excitement. Panting, he began, pointing his finger across the waving corn—

" I have watched him go," said he. " I have long waited for his exit. Time has crept on such tardy legs. I know him well," he remarked with a pitying smile; " as dull a dog as ever kept tame kennel. You are well rid of the fellow with his meek philosophy and his unblinking eyes. Faith, I would not have him trouble the ears of a maid for all the wealth of Prester John. A clucking barn-door cock, with emotions fit to scratch all day upon a dung-heap, and

not skill enough to discern the twinkling
of a diamond from the sad yellows of a
wheat-ear, wherewith to fill his stomach!''

Miranda stared at him, and burst into
tinkling laughter.

'' Good,'' says he, complacently, '' I see
you take him at his proper value. Pearls
have another destiny than to go for but-
tons on his sober sides. Such as he should
keep company with cold-visaged age. What
said the lover? Had he not arguments?''

''Oh, he had arguments to spare,'' she
laughed. '' Life was a deadly fustian-
coated thing to him. He pleaded for repose.''

'' Repose!'' he echoed. ''I pray I may
die when I come to think on repose with
any feeling but distaste. Repose! Oh,
yes; let them repose that love it; but they
shall not solicit into their stagnation aught
that is comely and vivacious. I know well
enough what life may be,'' he said, wag-

ging his head. "I have sounded all its mysteries. Take me for a pilot. I have tasted the sweet and the bitter"; and he sighed.

Miranda looked at him with pity. He was so young to have this sorrow in his heart. She sighed with him.

" But there are compensations," he went on presently. " One dies and the light goes out, but there remains still the beautiful world."

Miranda gazed round the valley.

" Will that suffice ?" she asked softly.

" Ah, no!" he cried; " a thousand noes. There is nothing will suffice save death. But life is laid upon us. What may we do? We take our pains and our pleasures; there is no rest. To rest were death in life. I could not sink into the moral worm that withdraws its blind head and wriggles into cover on the passage of a pain. Nay, I take life with my eyes open, though my back be bowed and my body bent, and though the ice encrust my soul. The grace of the day passes, but we are surely the happier even for that ephemeral sweetness."

"Yes; surely we are happier," assented Miranda, wondering at his fine words.

"And even when we think it not, there comes," said he, "some mitigation to Sorrow. There is the joy of Resignation; there is the delight of Sacrifice; and there is the sweetness of Remembered Pain ; and beyond all lies the gladness of Despair."

Miranda looked puzzled. She gazed at him inquiringly.

"You will think me absurd," said he; "but I talk out of my knowledge. I speak in sober words, as one upon whose hopes the grave has closed. Sorrow is a fire that refines; pain is a scourge that purifies. You are young, child, and go yet unscathed; but some day maybe—and that in but a little while—you may watch the sky grow black upon you, and feel the foundations of the earth totter, and your whole being will reel and burn and moan aloud to God within you. In such an hour you will remember and believe; and when you are crept into some insecure and windy refuge, trembling till the storm may pass, you will know that the blight of mortality is upon you. And you will finger your scars, and put your hands upon your wounds, realising that out of pain have you purchased knowledge, peace out of suffering, and out of despair hope."

The tears stood in Miranda's eyes. She laid a timid hand upon his arm. "Ah, how you have suffered!" she murmured.

He raised his sad gaze to hers and sighed. "I have wept out these eyes for want of such a one as you to succour me. Had but your tenderness and loving kindness been with me, the storm had surely passed in vain."

" Is it long gone ? " she asked gently.

" Some three months since," he answered; " and still is my heart sore within me. I dare not fancy how it will all end. The sun rises and I see it not; the air grows warm and I feel it not; the stars blink down upon me and I regard them not. Day passes after day, and night succeeds to night; yet is my long pain still with me, and I heed not the rolling years."

"'Tis but three months," she suggested.

" Three months are many years," he sighed.

Miranda looked at his misty blue eyes, and a thrill of pity pierced her soul.

" But you will be strong," she said; " you will pluck out the thorns from your heart, and it shall yet blossom again as the rose. You will not bow your head to trouble. I know so little, but surely again in the springtime you will find a fair flush upon your world."

The young man put out his hand and took hers.   He pressed it gently.

" 'Tis true," he said, " for others. They, indeed, may die with the waning moon, and be born again when she shows her new horns.   With each fresh week they may start anew into life.   Nay, even the hours are the measure of their fortunes.   But for me the spring is over and gone; out of the dead heart of the summer shall I snatch aught but withered leaves?   And shall I permit my own dead heart to take the dews and sunlight of an unavailing spring? Child, child, you know not, you cannot judge," and he patted softly on the hand he held between his fingers.

Miranda bent her head, and wept gently. He put his arm upon her shoulder, and looked into her eyes.

" Yes, there are other springs," said he, " but they are for you, and not for me. And still—and still your sweet voice comforts me, your dear tears console me. There is so much between us I would fain retain.''

Miranda stayed, reluctant, under his touch, and then, gently moving, would have withdrawn herself beyond him. But his hand held her fast; he tightened his clasp; a gulp of tears rolled into his throat.

'' Nay,'' he murmured; '' do not leave me so. Bear with me till this sorrow passes. 'Twill be gone in a little. See, the sky is clearing, and only on the horizon do the clouds lie black. Come, let me have your hand, and we will talk of what we know is true and beautiful—of life and love and the loveliness of life; for in you, dear child, all these are surely implicit.''

The red hung in Miranda's cheeks, and then went out slowly.

'' I love life,'' she answered in low tones, '' and I love the loveliness of life, but I know not why I love them.''

'' Because,'' said he, smiling, '' you yourself are informed with Love. Think you God made a maid so lovely and not for love? No; your arms were designed for a lover's necklace; your bosom was conceived for a lover's pillow; your lips for the sweet rest-ing-place of tired eyes, and you yourself for the delectation of many hapless wooers."

Miranda blushed, and stirred uncomfort-ably. Something in his rapturous fancy irked her, and yet it was surely right that one so buried in his distant sorrow should adjudge her thus. She conceived his kindly eyes upon her in a melancholy gaze, as of a brother who would fain reassure her out of his own troubled past. And then, she was sure, they passed away from her and across the valley where the golden mists were scat-tering, and lit upon the hill-tops somewhere far off, amid the kindly haze, and dwelt alone there with his sacred grief, as in a silent and inaccessible temple. She looked up in some awe, and found them fastened upon her with an ardent wistfulness. Her hand had fallen from his; he reached out, and seized it again.

"We have so much in common," he murmured. "My dear, the sweetness of those tremulous eyes!"

Miranda sharply pulled her fingers from him.

"Ah, sweet, be not so cruel," he pleaded; "you were not fashioned for disdain. Let me look. Yes, in those lamps of light I can behold my own face, drowned as in a pool. It shines therefrom, as starlight from a blue sky. Would God——"
He ended with a sigh.

"I will bid you good-day, Sir," says she; "the morning grows late."

"No, no!" he cried, catching at her hand.

Miranda stopped in wonder.

"And do you love me, then?" he asked in a cooing voice.

Miranda opened her mouth and stared.

" No," said she, shortly, after a pause.

He sighed musically, and his sigh ran like cold water down Miranda's back. He sighed again. Miranda turned, and in an instant, ere he was aware, flashed out upon him.

" And do you love me, then?" she mimicked, scorn in her cooing.

" Dear!" said he, and bent to kiss her hand. Miranda laughed.

" You love me, then?" she cried.

He made a motion of his hand, as though to banish an irrelevant thought.

" Why ply so bluntly?" he remarked, with some sad displeasure; " and why blow so coarsely? Love 'twixt man and maid— forgive me—should be as gentle as the breath of the zephyr, as light as the touch of warm sun upon the rose. There is no need of terms. Heart looks to heart and holds communion silently. Nay, but the fault was mine. I ask your pardon. I put too gross a question to you. Let us rather linger in this delicious incertitude all day. The morning is young; we have the fields before us; let us wander there, and you shall pluck the flowers and idly weave a garland for your head, while I look on and smile, a bird singing in my heart, unquestioned, standing alone within a maze of ways, yet undismayed, knowing this only, that the full glory of love is not to know, and the full flower of life is expectation.''

" You talk great nonsense, sir," says she.

" Ah, no," he broke in. " Believe me——" But before the flash in her eyes he paused.

" Ere you put tongue to further follies," says she, " listen. Out of my ignorance shall I instruct your wisdom. You have too soft a heart for this rude world. I pity you. Your soul is like a flying bird, ever at the rough mercy of the fowler. Boom! goes the gun, and down it falls, winged and whimpering at her feet. Why, she has never so much as to put her finger on the lock, but you will fall fluttering at the mere glint of it. You have whole seas of sentiment within your eyes. Lord! how you would weep! You would drown out this valley in a week, and flood my garden for a fallen sparrow. Tears! Tears are your finery. You bedeck yourself with them, and strut among your acquaintances the proudest wight of all. You cull posies of sentiment by every wayside. Not a day but you will have a fresh desire, own a fresh sorrow, and crown a fresh conquest. Victor and victim! I salute your immortal youth. Other men have died for love, but to you alone has it been vouchsafed to live for it. So, as you may cry and mourn and sigh and go forlorn, touch delicate hands, and interchange the soft felicities of affection, you will walk in a whirl of gaiety to your grave. Sir, you would bury a thousand loves with delirious delight. Oh, you are too fastidious; you exact too much. It were surely wiser to fill your hours more economically with griefs. They will not outlast you. Sorrow abides but for a night. Have you never laughed? Did joy never wear any face for you save that of bereavement? Did ever your pulse flow faster save at the prospect of sepulture? I beseech you to adventure more. Believe me, there are fields of sweet emotion as yet untrodden of your feet. Come, for an experiment, stay a whole week with your heart's delight; I can foresee for you new and strange sensations. You shall decay beautifully. This rare and lovely sentiment of yours will turn all manner of raw colours. It will shine rank, and smell stale; it will take on all the hues of swift corruption. But think on them, and should they fall and you exhaust the universe, why, there is always the river, and the rain of tears upon self-contemplated suicide. You shall stand over the brink, and pause, and murmur to the trees, and roll your eyes to heaven, and look down with compassion upon your elegant limbs, so soon to toss among the graceless weeds. And I, if you will, shall bear you witness, and copy your fair sentences into some white book, and send them down the ages, engraven above a golden heart. Oh, I will frame you an admirable, a most pitiful epitaph. Nay, but I mistake, for surely it were meeter writ from your own dictation."

She paused for want of breath, and the young man raised his hand in a manner of deprecation.

"It is enough," he said, and sighed, "I have mistaken. Forgive me the lack of judgment. Had I regarded sufficiently the tip of your nose, indeed I had not blundered." Miranda's fingers went to her face. "I had thought you endowed with the qualities of sympathy. But," he shrugged his shoulders, "one blunders still. Indeed, one blunders after many blunders. You are too pert and young. You put life to the coarse edge of fact. Believe me, you were better living in ideals. One buys facts by the gross, and at so many pence. The ideal we snatch from the empyrean. You shall go your way, and I mine." Miranda curtsied. "I bear you no malice for your wanton tongue. Child, you will learn wisdom, and come to regard affection."

With that, he made her a great bow, and, turning slowly, made off with a heavy appearance of sorrow. At the corner of the hedge he stopped, glanced over his shoulder, raised his hat, and sighed loudly.

Miranda stood watching his receding figure with something between a smile and a frown upon her dainty face.

V. LACK-LUSTRE VIRTUE

Miranda put a finger to the tip of her nose and frowned.

" 'Tis false," she murmured querulously; " it is straight enough in all conscience. Oh, I abhor spite," and, shrugging her shoulders angrily, she ran lightly through the green corn down upon the little wood below.

Here a pleasant brook fretted over tiny falls, and curled in eddies round large, smooth pebbles. The morning sun struck a slant through the willows, and patches of blue sky beamed up from the depths of the shallow water. Miranda stepped upon the frail bridge and leaned over the handrail. The mirror below her was full of wavering shadows and grey light. The stream trickled coolly in that secluded dell, and Miranda's face was flushed and hot with her haste. The breeze went softly through the tresses of her hair. Miranda glanced along the shelving banks to where a grassy knoll jutted forth upon a corner of the brook. She left the bridge, and walking to the spot, looked down upon the water. The dell was silent.

Her eyes flew swiftly this way and that, in furtive diffidence, and then, fast as a flash, she slipped her shoes from under her feet, and flung her hosen down, and, dropping upon the knoll, dabbled her white feet in the current. The water washed about her ankles gently, and she watched the curves in her high arches dissolve and change and waver in the eddies. How translucent was the stream! How still and sweet the air! She bent forward and regarded her face in the deep pool. Suddenly, and with a little gasp of terror, she found the earth slipping from her. She threw herself back and clutched wildly at the grass. She felt the water creeping above her ankles. A cry escaped her, and on the next instant two hands were clasped beneath her arms, and she was swiftly drawn into safety, and lay high upon the grass upon her back. Miranda sat up, and looking round met the bashful eyes of a youth. At once his gaze dropped, and he fumbled his hands together, shifting from foot to foot.

"I beg your pardon," said he, "but you——"

"Oh, you are very kind," said Miranda earnestly. "I thank you, Sir. Another moment and I had been lost."

"It is but shallow," he mumbled smiling, and bit his nail.

Miranda laughed awkwardly. "Oh, but thank you, Sir," she said, "you are very good."

"'Twas but my duty," he stammered, and looked away, frowning at the trees;

" anyone would have done more for you,"
he added, blushing.

Miranda's gaze went down her gown, and
hastily she plucked her bare feet under her
skirt.   There fell a long silence, during
which he fidgeted with the stalks of the
bracken, and Miranda beat her fingers impatiently upon her knee.

"Heavens! will the man never speak or
go?" thought Miranda.   " The sun shines
bright, and the birds sing sweet," says she;
" we shall soon be in full spring."

" Very bright," said he, starting; " very
sweet," he added, and " 'twill rain by
nightfall," he ventured, cocking his eye at
the sky.

" Ah!" said Miranda, fanning herself
with her hat.

Again a pause ensued. The young man
shuffled on his feet; he whistled gently.
Miranda yawned and drummed her fingers
faster on her knee. She gave a little cough.

" I fear," he stuttered, " you will grow cold upon the moist slope. The sun has little power upon the dews within this shade. If I might beg——"

Approaching, he held out a vague hand. Miranda shut her mouth with a snap.

" I thank you," she said, with scorn, " but the dew delights me. I am never content save upon damp grass."

" I—I crave your pardon," he besought her. " I—I—fancied——"

" I hate a fool!" quoth Miranda to herself, in anger.

His eyes wandered to the stream. " Why, there are your shoes," says he,. brightening, " and your hosen. Pray——"

He made a hasty movement forward.

" I beg you will be at no trouble for me," cried Miranda, flaming. " Suffer me, at least, I pray you, the liberty to dispose of my own apparel. I am no child at nurse."

He drew back, red and frightened, and Miranda, breathless, curled her feet closer beneath her gown. He watched her face askance. She bit her lips.

"He is only a fool; but I hate a fool," said she.

Miranda sighed. He glanced at her anxiously.

"And you think it will rain?" she asked.

"I'll swear it will," he cried eagerly, and waited, open-mouthed, upon her condescension.

"I wonder," said Miranda thoughtfully.

"But the sky is red," he panted.

"I have my doubts," said Miranda sagely, shaking her head. "The wood obscures the heaven. How is it possible to tell?"

"Indeed——" he began.

"Nay," she interrupted; "but from the cornfield yonder you could descry with certainty, and I should be reassured."

"I can see the cornfield through the trees," he answered, "and the sun shines red above the hedges."

Miranda shrugged her shoulders petulantly.

"What sound was that?" she said. "Surely some animal. I hate a cow!" she exclaimed. "Oh, Sir, pray run and see!"

"'Tis no cow," he replied stolidly. "I know the fields by heart, and there is never a cow within two miles."

"There is many a fool," said Miranda bitterly.

"Aye, to be sure," he assented easily; "and many a 'sinner, moreover," he added thoughtfully.

"I think I prefer a sinner," said Miranda vehemently.

"The sinner for me, too," he agreed cheerfully.

Miranda put out her tongue at the grass.

Idly he broke the bark of a silver birch. Miranda uttered an exclamation of anger. He turned.

" I beg your pardon," said he. " I did not catch your words, but I do assure you that if there is aught I can do will——"

Miranda's temper burst its bonds. " Nothing in the world," she said, in sarcasm; " nothing in life for me, save only that you will leave me to enjoy my solitude."

He started, stammered half a sentence, took off his hat, mopped his face, and, tumbling over a creeper, set off. Miranda's heart pricked her pride. He looked forlorn, and he had done his best in honest stupidity.

" Stay!" she called impetuously. He tarried in wonder. " I meant no unkindness, Sir." He came stumbling back. " I have an intermittent trick of petulance." The light beamed in a broad grin upon his face.

Miranda shivered. He sat down squat upon the bracken. Miranda groaned.

"I wondered at your cruel words," he began slowly. "Somehow they fitted ill your face, which is"—he blushed—"the sweetest I have seen."

"Oh, you are rash," said Miranda scornfully; "I dare swear that one with so much knowledge as yourself has weltered among scores of pretty faces."

"Indeed——" he cried, but she broke in upon his protest.

"For myself, I lay no claim to beauty; let others flaunt their titles as they will. I am well enough, no doubt. I have the face of youth, and my eyes have no squint in them. But I am assured you have seen many pretty maidens."

"That is so," he cried eagerly, "and this the prettiest."

Miranda smiled. "You do your friends a harsh injustice," she answered. "I have

my years to my credit, and no more, which
is a virtue through which each must passage.
And what, indeed, is beauty, if all be
told ?''

'' Beauty ? It is a pearl,'' he gasped, and
suddenly swallowed his emotion with a gulp.

'' I set no value upon pearls,'' said Miranda sedately. '' Let others if they will.
While the world swings on, folly will ring
her bells, fools gape, and gossips chatter.''

He watched her ardently, and sidling a
step nearer, resumed his argument.

'' You cannot tell,'' he said, '' with how
full a heart a man regards beauty. The
tears start in his eyes at the sight, his breath
catches, and his legs fall to trembling.''

'' Ah! is it so ?'' asked Miranda indifferently.

He rolled himself upon his stomach, and
looked up into her face.

'' It is with me,'' he said earnestly. His
gaze embarrassed her. She turned her head

away. " I have long wondered about this love," he stammered, " and now I know."

Miranda looked round at him quickly.

" What is it like ? " she asked, with some interest.

Abashed, he thrust his fingers through his hair. " I—I beg your pardon," he stuttered; " but I have scarce the wherewithal to clothe my feelings. It makes me—'tis like a—oh, I feel—indeed, and I would do anything in your behalf," he concluded bravely.

Miranda stared at him a second, and then smiled softly. He sprawled so ungainly; he lay a huge hulk of ineptitudes; his large blue eyes were watered with affection.

" You are very good," she murmured.

" 'Tis no goodness," he averred stoutly, " but out of the very bottom of indulgent selfishness. I would sacrifice worlds for you."

Miranda glanced at him slyly. " Would you drown ? " she asked.

He nodded.

" Would you surrender me forever ?"

He hesitated.

" Would you sell your soul for me ?"

He knit his brows into a frown of puzzlement.

" Why," cried she, " you would never surely steal to set me smiling ?"

He shook his head thoughtfully. " No," he replied. " 'Twould be a wrong you would not ask of me."

" And if I did ?" she insisted.

He searched her face, and then, " I would hire someone else for the job," he declared, with a sigh.

Miranda lay back on the turf, and shook with laughter. Suddenly she sat up; in a flash the laughter ceased, and red and white in turn she tucked her bare feet beneath her gown again.

" I trust," said he anxiously, " that you have not hurt yourself."

"Oh, no," she replied coldly. "Pray continue. Your philosophy was most entertaining. You make a scruple of theft, I understand. But you could love me to distraction. Oh, yes. You will pull down the world for me, an you do it not by your own hand. You will meet lions, an you can find another to replace you. You will swear and forswear, and break through the decalogue, if you can do all these things by substitute. Yours is a wonderful sense of passion, so new, so strange, so masterful."

The young man nodded his head sagely. " 'Tis marvellous what change Love will bring to a man, but," he added doubtfully, " I would not break through the decalogue. I dare not have another's blood upon me. Oh, there are many things one dare not do, nor would you ask them. Why do I talk so wildly ? I am content to love you, if you will suffer me."

He leaned forward and took her hand

awkwardly, looking the while into her face with bashful affection. She snapped her hand away, and laughed impatiently.

"Oh, you are too good, fair Sir," she cried. "I am not worthy of your devout devotion. I? I have sins enough upon my head, God wot, but none so great as this unequal partnership would be. You are too virtuous for such as I. You are too much composed of discreet renunciations. Renounce once more, and save your soul alive. Mine is the waywardness of the wild cat; I have the passions of the desperado. I break through a commandment daily. I am right to my hair in sins. Should I repent I should need an acre of sackcloth and gallons of ashes. But I do not; thank the Lord, I shall not. I am stark in my vices. I complete them with exultation; I plan them with rebellious joys. I am a fiend in a fair wig, a ghoul in a white gown. To love me is to love perdition."

He stared at her dumbly, and withdrew a pace.

"Indeed," said she, "you have every reason for your fears. I fear myself. O' nights I lie awake and think of devilments; they float through my dreams. I pinch myself in wonder if I be really human. There is no audacity I could not dare, no shame to cause me blink."

He shuffled a little further away.

"Come, come," she cried, "begone ere I break out upon you. I have the very deuce of a temper. For you and yours I see the happy valleys open; for me is the rude path among the mountains. Get you gone, then, Sir, to your happiness and the sweet maid that awaits you. Mine is the bitter, narrow road to Hell!"

She rose to her feet and pointed at him mockingly with her finger. The young man turned, and casting back one glance across his shoulder, scampered heavily through the undergrowth without a word, and disappeared into the wood.

Miranda stopped, breathless. " I believe he took me for the Devil," she said, and laughed. " But oh, the prickles!" she cried, drawing in her breath and grimacing. She flung herself upon the ground and rubbed her pretty feet.

Miranda reached for her hose. " 'Twas difficult," she murmured; " 'twas very difficult; but at last—at last!"

VI. THE ROSES

Miranda crossed the bridge and struck into the little copse.

" To think," said she, " that Love is that! To think that I should be loved like that! She smiled at the recollection, and then sighed. " Oh, for my garden!" she exclaimed wearily. " There is no such thing as Love. There are only the flowers, and the spring, and the sunshine.''

The thicket was close-set with trees; the way was rough and thorny.

'' I *will* break through,'' cried Miranda angrily, and tore the briers viciously from her gown. As she was bent thus lowly, and ere she raised her head, she was aware of someone standing by. A little shadow of fear sailed across her heart. She started, and looking up met the eyes of a young man.

Miranda looked down: her heart throbbed fast; the fragrance of the wild roses stole through her senses. Miranda looked up: the sunlight flashed and sparkled on the green thicket.

'' Pray give me leave,'' said the stranger, and dropped upon his knees.

Miranda's bosom rose and fell as he disentangled her frock from the thorns.

'' I thank you, Sir,'' she said timidly, when he was got upon his feet again.

He laughed, and looked at her with smiling eyes. Their glances met, and both fell on the instant. In the silence upon that the stream wimpled loud behind them. Miranda took her gown in hand and moved gently away. The young man raised his face and watched her go. She reached a little bend in the pathway, and he stirred.

" I pray you," he called, " pardon my interruption, but the brake is grown thick and the passage narrow. You were better upon the roadway."

" I have no fears," said she, " and the road is adust and dreary."

She vanished round the point. He sped after her to the corner.

" I pray you," he called, " forgive my foolish importunity, but the hill beyond is steep and crowned with thorns."

" I have climbed it often," she responded, " and in the spring daffodils grow upon the slopes."

He bit his finger meditatively as he watched her. Suddenly—

" Let me help you, then," he cried.

" Help ?" she echoed, and hesitated.

He pushed aside the branches of the nut-tree. " See," he said, " they would close against a girlish arm. They are in a sworn conspiracy against maidens. 'Tis only the strong hand of the woodman bends them to his will."

" Are you a woodman ?" she asked demurely.

He shook his head, laughing. " Nay, but I have learned a trick to teach the surly louts civility." A branch leapt forth and struck him on the cheek. A stain of red sprang up to meet it.

" Oh!" cried Miranda, in distress.

" 'Tis spite—they rankle," said he, with a merry smile; " see, how they would entreat you. But they shall know their master, and bow to a lady." He swept them back with a movement of his long arm. " Pass, pass," he said; " they cringe, and dare not."

Miranda looked, and bent her head. " 'Tis closer than I had thought," she murmured, as she disappeared beneath the archway of his arms.

He followed, and she turned to him in despair.

" I was a little, wanton fool," she said plaintively. " How is it possible to pierce this thicket ?"

With a laugh he threw himself against the brushwood, and a passage slowly opened.

" I thank you, Sir," she said softly. " You are too kind to a wilful maid."

" 'Tis worse and worse," he said, surveying the tangle breathlessly. " But the hill slopes lie beyond. Come." He took her hand. Miranda breathed hard. She fluttered after him beneath the coppice.

" My hair!" she cried suddenly, in a sharp note of pain.

He stopped in a moment and begged a thousand pardons. A brown tress glimmered in the clutch of an alder. He put up his hand and pulled.

" I pray you, Sir, be gentle," she murmured distressfully.

He invoked a thousand murrains on himself. " I must come closer," said he.

" I think," she murmured, " that I myself "—she shrank from him and gave her head a shake, stopping with a little gasp.

" I fear 'tis too secure," said he, and drew gently nearer.

He peered into the tangle; his breath moved in her hair; his fingers were entwined in the brown tresses. Miranda's heart beat quickly. With a deft twist of his hand she was free.

" I thank you, Sir," again quoth she. She sped along the pathway into the open, where the track ran lazily up the slope.

" I thank you," she repeated, and put out her hand, with a bow. He took it, bowing in answer, and his face fell.

" But there is the hill," he said dolefully. " I may not leave you yet."

" An excellent hill to climb upon a soft morning," says she. " Good-bye."

" Were you to stumble——" he began anxiously.

" I should pick myself up and laugh," she concluded promptly.

He sighed, and looked back at the copse. She moved away a pace or two, and pausing, glanced at him. Before his gaze her own sank, and again her heart swung faster.

" 'Tis a rough way," he said sadly.

" 'Tis true," she murmured, " there is the quarry."

He climbed towards her. " I will see you past it," he said firmly.

Miranda answered nothing, but went slowly onwards. He leapt above her, and, leaning back, gave her his hand. " There is a huge boulder here," he explained.

" I had forgot," she murmured.

He pulled her over the obstruction.

" Good Heavens!" he cried, " the gorse! We had forgot also the gorse."

She surveyed the gorse with dismay. The bushes rose waist high.

" How stupid!" said Miranda pettishly. " They should have been cut down."

" There's never a path runs through them," he said triumphantly.

" We must go back," said Miranda with a sigh.

" There is the thicket again," he cried with jubilation.

" True," she murmured.

There was a moment's pause, and then:

" I must carry you through the gorse!" he exclaimed, with ill-repressed exultation.

Miranda flushed. " Indeed, I can walk," said she coldly. She took a step into the midst, and the thorns pierced her ankles. Miranda kept her lips close, and took another step. The thorns crept higher.

" Oh!" cried Miranda in the dismay of pain.

" Let me have your arm," he said, " and we shall help each other."

" No, no," said Miranda dolefully; " it hurts, it hurts; I will go back."

" You cannot," said he.

Miranda frowned. " I will sit down."

" You dare not," said he joyfully.

Miranda's head sank; the tears came into her eyes.

" Lean upon me," he whispered.

Miranda leant. He put his arms beneath her, and, disengaging the thorns from her skirt, lifted her from her feet.

" Oh," she exclaimed. " How dare you ? "

" Hush," he whispered, " 'twill be over soon. Shut your eyes and hold your breath, so shall you never set eyes upon my horrid face. 'Tis but a horse, an ass, an elephant that carries you over a difficult crossing."

Miranda said not a word. He jogged heavily along amid the gorse. He stumbled. Miranda clutched his shoulder tightly. He stopped and bent over her.

" Put me down," she said imperiously, shutting her eyes.

He set her down. Miranda smoothed her gown. She turned her pink face from him.

" I am much in your debt, Sir," she said, " and now I will wish you good-day."

" There is yet the quarry," he objected.

Miranda winced. He walked by her side, and in silence they clambered into the quarry and out upon the further side. In silence they reached the garden. Miranda turned and thrust out her hand for the third time.   His eyes were fastened upon her throat.

" And now," says she primly, " 'tis really good-day.   I do not know how I may repay you for your goodness.   But——"

" With a rose," he stammered.

Miranda glanced demurely around.

" There is none by," she answered.

" 'Tis at your throat," he said, " if I may make so bold——"

" Oh, if you will," said she with indifference.   " I was about to have discarded it."

She plucked it from her neck and held it forth.   He stuck it in the lapel of his coat. She opened the little gate and entered the garden.   The first turning of the pathway hid the stranger from her view.   She lingered and stooped over a rose-bush.   A flood of new fragrance rushed through her senses.   Something sang in her blood.   A loud knock sounded in her heart.   Miranda started, and the young man stood before her.

" I crave your indulgence," he stammered, " but I have forgot the hour, and it is now late, and I must needs be thinking of my destination."

Miranda crossed to the sun-dial on the lawn.

" 'Tis only noon," she said. " 'Tis very late," she added quickly.

" Ah, noon," he responded; " yes, noon, of course. How foolish!" and walked back slowly towards the gate.

Miranda bent over the roses, and the perfume filled her with an ecstasy till now unknown. The garden was ringing with song, and her body thrilled with a passionate sympathy till now unfelt. Again at her heart a loud noise sounded, and again she started.

" 'Tis very stupid in me," laughed the stranger, in embarrassment. " My wits have wandered. But is it Tuesday or surely Wednesday to-day ?"

Miranda reflected. " 'Twas Monday yesterday," she answered thoughtfully.

" Ah, then," said he sagely, " 'tis Tuesday to-day, and 'twill be Wednesday to-morrow." He moved away again reluctantly. " A fine shining day," he called, " and admirable weather for the flowers."

" 'Twill rain, maybe," said Miranda, glancing at the sky.

" No doubt," he said, and lingered.

Miranda stooped over the roses. He melted slowly round the bend in the pathway. The sunlight flashed upon the lilac, and Miranda's heart danced up and down tumultuously. A shadow fell across the bed.
· " If you said noon," said the stranger, " I could reach the Vale ere one ?"

" Why, yes," she answered, " if you should start at once."

" 'Tis time, indeed, to go," said he absently.

" 'Tis certainly time," said Miranda. A

cloud blew over the sunlight, and the roses blurred before her eyes.

There was a long silence. Miranda sighed, and turning, moved slowly up the pathway. At the distance of ten steps she stopped and glanced down at her shoe. The latchet trailed upon the ground, and, with a pout, she bent to lace it up. But the young man was before her, and, kneeling upon the ground, looked up in her face.

" 'Tis my last privilege ere I go," he pleaded.

Miranda looked away, but, for all she saw, the garden was a desert. It seemed he was a long time at her shoe, but the garden was so large and beautiful that she had forgot the minutes. And all the time her heart was thumping in her side, and the door was creaking on its latch. He rose and stood before her.

" The Vale," said he, " is far distant."

" 'Tis very far," she answered gently.

" And the sun is past noon," he continued.

" 'Tis late," she assented.

" 'Twere better I should wait and take refreshment ere I go," said he.

" No doubt, 'twere wiser," she murmured, looking down.

" I shall be very lonely," said he.

" 'Tis lonely to be alone," she whispered.

He put out his arm. She stared at the roses. How they blew. How red they grew. How their hearts fluttered. How sweet and fragrant smelled the garden.

" I were not alone with Love," he said in low tones.

" With Love!" she murmured to the roses.

The clouds drifted from the face of the sun, and the light streamed down upon them. Larks sprang warbling to Heaven. The garden awoke into light and music. In the pause something drew Miranda's eyes to his face; his eyes were deep in dew. Miranda felt her own grow misty. A surge of tears rose up from her heart; the swing-gates of her soul flew open, and through the portals, ere she was aware, there passed swiftly—Something—Something—she knew not what.

She gave a little sob. The young man put his arms about her.

The Dead Wall

The dawn stared raw and yellow out of the east at Rosewarne. Its bleak and ugly face smouldered through morose vapours. The wind blew sharp against the windows, shaking them in their casements. The prospect from that lonely chamber overawed him with menace; it glowered upon him. The houses in the square, wrapped in immitigable gloom, were to him ominous memorials of death. They frightened him into a formless panic. Anchored in that soundless sea, they terrified him with their very stillness. In dreary ranks they rose, a great high wall of doom, lifting their lank chimneys to the dreadful sky. They obsessed him with forebodings to which he could put no term, for which he could find no reason. Shrouded under its great terror, his poor mind fell into deeper depression under the influence of those malign and ugly signals. He strove to withdraw his thoughts and direct them upon some different subject. He wrenched them round to the contemplation of his room, his walls, his wife. A dull pain throbbed in the back of his head. He repeated aloud the topics upon which he would have his mind revolve, but the words rang in his ears without meaning. He touched the pictures on the wall, he spoke their names, he covered his face and strained hard to recapture coherent thought. The subjects mocked him: they were too nimble and elusive for his tired brain; they danced out of reach, and he followed blindly till a deeper darkness fell. They grew faint and shadowy like wraiths in a mist, and he pursued the glancing shadows. Finally, his brain grew blank; it was as if consciousness had lapsed; and he found himself regarding a fly that crawled upon the pane. Outside lay the oppression of that appalling scene that horrified him—he knew not why.

Rosewarne was growing used to these nervous exhibitions. This unequal struggle had been repeated through many weeks, but he had always so far come out of it with personal security. The dread that some day he would fail continually haunted him, and increased the strain of the conflict. He wondered what lay at the back of this horrible condition, and shuddered as he wondered. And he knew now that he must not let himself adrift, but must allay the devils by every means. He broke into a whistle, and moved about the room carelessly. It was a lively stave from the streets that his lips framed, but it conveyed to him no sense of sound. He perambulated the chamber with a false air of cheerfulness. He eyed the bed with his head askew, winking as if to share a jest with it. He patted the pillows, arranging and disarranging them in turn. He laughed softly, merrily, emptily. He seized the dumbbells from the mantelpiece and whirled them about his head; he chafed his hands, he rubbed his flesh. Little by little the blood moved with more content through his body, and the pulse of his heart sank slowly.

Outside, the dawn brightened and the wind came faster. Rosewarne looked forth and nodded; then he turned and left the room, his face flashing as he passed the mirror, like the distempered face of a corpse. Across the landing he paused before a door, and, bending to the keyhole, listened; little low sounds of life came to his ears, and suddenly his haggard face crowded with emotions. He rose and softly descended the stairs to his study. The house lay in the quiet of sleep, and within the solitude of that rich room he, too, was as still as the sleepers. The inferior parts of the window formed a blind of stained glass, but the grey light flowed through the upper panes into a magnificent wilderness. The cold ashes of the fire, by which he had sat at his task late into the morning, lay still within the grate. The little ensigns of a human presence, the scattered papers, the dirty hearth, all the instruments of his work, looked mean and squalid within the spacious dignity of that high room. He lit the gas and sat down to his table, moving his restless fingers among the papers. It was as if his members arrogantly claimed their independence, and refused the commands of a weak brain. His mind had abrogated. His hands shifted furtively like the hands of a pickpocket: they wandered among the papers and returned to him. The clock droned out the hour slowly, and at that he started, shook his wits together, and began in haste to turn about the documents. He knew now the sheet of which he had sent his hands in quest. Large and blue and awful, it had been his ghost throughout the night. He could see the figures scrawled upon it in his own tremulous writing, rows upon rows of them, thin and sparse and self-respecting at the top, but to the close, fevered, misshapen, and reckless, fighting and jostling in a crowd for space upon the page. He laid his hand upon the horrible thing; he opened his ledgers; and sat deciphering once more his own ruin.

The tragedy lay bare to his shrinking eyes; it leaped forth at him from the blurred and confused figures. There was no need to rehearse them; he had reiterated them upon a hundred scrolls in a hundred various ways these many weeks. They had become his enemies, to deceive whom he had invoked the wreck of a fine intelligence. He had used all the wiles and dodges of a cunning mind to entrap them to his service. He had spent a weary campaign upon them, storming them with fresh troops of figures, deploying and ambuscading with all the subterfuge of a subtle business mind. But there now, as at the outset of his hopeless fight, the issue remained unchanged; the terrible sum of his sin abode, unsubtracted, undivided, unabridged. As he regarded it at this moment it seemed to assume quickly a vaster proportion. His crime cried out upon him, calling for vengeance in his ears. Seizing a pen, eagerly, vacantly, he set forth anew to recompose the items.

Rosewarne worked on for a couple of hours, holding his quivering fingers to the paper by the sheer remnants of his will. His brain refused its offices, and he stumbled among the numerical problems with false and blundering steps. To add one sum to another he must ransack the litter of his mind; the knowledge that runs glibly to the tongue of a child he must rediscover by persistent and arduous concentration. But still he kept his seat, and jotted down his cyphers. About him the house stirred slowly; noises passed his door and faded; the grim and yellow sun rose higher and struck upon the table, contending with the gaslight. But Rosewarne paid no heed; he wrestled with his numb brain and his shivering fingers, wrestled to the close of the page; where once more the hateful figures gleamed in bold ink, menacing and blinking, his old ghost renewed and invested with fresh life.

The pen dropped from his hand, his head fell upon his arms, and as he lay in that helpless attitude of despair that protests not, of misery that can make no appeal, the door fell softly open and his wife entered.

" Freddy, whatever are you doing here like this ? " she said, with surprise in her voice. " Have you gone to sleep ? "

Rosewarne lifted his head sharply and turned to her. Athwart the pallor of his face gleamed for an instant a soft flush of pleasure, and his dull eyes lit up with affection.

" I was doing some work, Dorothy," said he, " and I was tired."

Mrs. Rosewarne took a step nearer. Her fine grey eyes regarded him with wonder and with inquiry, and in her voice a little impatience mingled with a certain kindliness.

" It's very absurd your working like this," she said, " and in this cold room without a fire! Aren't you coming to breakfast ? "

Rosewarne got up from his chair. " Why, yes," he laughed. " Of course. I didn't realise it was ready. Oh, Dolly dear," he paused and put his hand to his head with a look of perplexity; then his face lightened. " Dolly, I've got something for you."

" For me!" she asked, and the curve of her lips drooped in a pretty smile of curiosity.

He fumbled in a drawer and withdrew a packet.

"Yes, darling. You know what day it is. It's your birthday, and you're twenty——"

"Oh, for goodness' sake, Freddy, don't," she interrupted with a touch of impatience; and then opening the packet examined the contents with care. A light dawned in her eyes. "How very pretty! I was in need of a bracelet. Freddy, you are a good boy. But come, you mustn't catch cold. Come into the dining-room, and get warm, you simpleton."

She patted him softly on the head, and fell again to the scrutiny of her present. Rosewarne did not move, but watched her, smiling. "Aren't you coming?" she asked, looking up at last.

His eyes met hers and pleaded with them dumbly, but she made no sign, returning once more to her jewels.

" Isn't it worth a kiss, Dolly ?" he asked softly.

Mrs. Rosewarne looked at him vaguely. "What! Oh, well, yes, if you like, I suppose." She bent towards him, and he touched her cheek gently. "But it was very nice of you to think of me," she said, withdrawing. "Come to breakfast now."

Rosewarne followed her into the breakfast-room, with a fresh access of impotence. He fumbled with his chair; the napkin fluttered out of his fingers; he pulled a plate to him, and the silver rattled under his clumsy action; a fork clattered to the floor. Mrs. Rosewarne winced.

"How very stupid you are to-day, Freddy!" she said pettishly.

He laughed a short, meaningless laugh, and begged her pardon. Her movements were full of gentle grace; her breath came easily and with the best breeding. Her teacup tinkled sweetly, and only that and the soft sussurra of her sleeves marked her stately presence at the table. She looked at the bracelet comfortably, and lifted her cup to her lips. Rosewarne glanced at her timidly. The sickly light shone clear upon the fine contours of her placid face; the evil magic of that dreary day was transmuted upon her hair. She set down her cup and met his eyes.

"What a dreadful colour you are!" she said critically. The ghastly yellow of his face repelled her. "I wish you would get better, and not rise at such ridiculous hours."

"I slept ill, Dolly," he answered with a faint smile. He resumed his breakfast feverishly. The knuckles of his hands seemed to stand out awkwardly; his elbows waggled; he mouthed at his food in a frightened fashion.

"Good heavens, Freddy," cried his wife, wrinkling her nose in distaste, "why do you eat like that? It's more like an animal than a human being. Your manners are becoming perfectly awful.''

He started and dropped his knife. '' What the devil does it matter how I eat ?'' he exclaimed angrily. '' You—you——'' His ideas faded from him, and he sat staring at her in vacant indignation. Then he put his hand to his head. '' Oh, forgive me, Dolly; forgive me, please. I'm tired and——''

'' My dear man,'' broke in Mrs. Rosewarne coldly, '' if you will make yourself ill, what can you expect ?'' She unfolded a morning paper and ran her eyes down the columns; Rosewarne sat looking across the room into the fire. Suddenly she called to him in a new voice. '' Mr. Maclagan came to town yesterday, Freddy, and paid a visit to Downing Street.''

'' Yes ?'' he said, starting again.

She drew down the paper and looked at him over the edge, her eyes filled with some excitement.

" Do you hear, Freddy dear ? Now is your chance to make the arrangement final."

He gazed at her, his face contorted in a desperate attempt to concentrate his thoughts upon her words. What was she saying ? And what did it mean ?

" Freddy, don't you hear ?" she cried again in a voice in which impatience blended with a certain eagerness. She leaned forward and put a hand upon his arm. He clutched at it feverishly with his fingers. " Lord Hambleton is favourable, I know, and it only remains to secure Maclagan," she went on quickly. " He, you know, was inclined to agree when you saw him before. I'm sure that the nail is ready for the hammer. There is South Wiltshire, where you are known, and no one yet settled upon by the Party. See, dear; you must call on him to-day, and that, with another cheque for the Party, should place the matter beyond doubt. Freddy! Freddy! Don't you hear what I'm saying ? For goodness' sake, don't look like a corpse, if you are ill.''

'' Yes, yes, Dolly,'' said Rosewarne hurriedly.

'' And for the love of decency, don't Dolly me,'' said Mrs. Rosewarne with a petulant movement of her shoulders. '' It's bad enough to have to answer to an elderly Quaker name like Dorothy.''

Rosewarne got up from the table. '' For God's sake, be civil to me, if you can't be kind,'' he said sharply. She regarded him coldly. '' What is it you want ?'' he asked.

Mrs. Rosewarne rapped her knuckles angrily upon the table.

'' I imagined we had made that pretty clear between us long ago,'' she said with a sarcastic emphasis; '' we agreed that you were to go into Parliament, and we laid our plans to that end. The only thing wanting was the particular seat, and now it's found you ask me what I'm talking about.''

She looked at him with placid disdain. Rosewarne shuddered; he remembered now, as in a dream, the ambitions she had formed for him.

"No, no, dear," he said. "Tell me. It's all right. I'll see Lord—Lord Hambleton. The——"

Mrs. Rosewarne's expression turned swiftly to complacency.

"No," she said, "leave him to me, Freddy. I shall see him this afternoon at the Charters's. You must see Maclagan to-day, and we'll meet and talk the matter over at dinner."

She smiled upon him with a tolerant air of patronage. Rosewarne stood by the window, restlessly twitching his fingers.

"You will not be in to lunch?" he asked, dully.

"No; I'm going to the Charters's. We have each a long day before us. It's a sort of crisis in our lives. I'm tired of this undistinguished competence.   Any one can be the partner in a bank.   It is the House that opens the gate to success."

She rose and swept her skirts behind her with a motion of her arm.   She regarded herself in the mirror with a face of satisfaction, directing with nimble fingers an errant lock of her hair.

" And now you'll be off, I suppose," she said, and turned on him laughing.   " Well, Freddy, pluck up your heart and speak your best; you have a tongue as neat as any one when you like.   Don't wear so lugubrious a countenance, dear—come!"

She kissed him lightly on the forehead, laying her hands on his shoulders, her eyes sparkling with excitement.   Rosewarne put out his arms and caught her.   His eyes devoured her.   " Kiss me again, Dolly," he sputtered.   " Kiss me again.   Kiss me on the lips."

She laughed, a faint colour rose in her

cheeks, and she struggled in his clutch. "Dolly, Dolly!" he pleaded. A frown of embarrassment gathered in her forehead.

"Do let me go," she said sharply.

He obeyed; his arms fell to his sides; wistfully he watched her withdraw. Stately in her flowing, rustling robes, receding from him, she sailed through the doorway, and with the loss of that fine vision the light and the flush fell from him, and all that remained was an ignoble figure with discoloured cheeks and sunken head. In that moment and with the chill of that departing grace fresh upon him, he regarded his tragic position plainly and without illusion. The poor rags of his last unvoiced hopes dropped from his outcast soul. He had deferred the story of his ruin, in part out of shame, but much, too, out of pity, and because of some shreds of confidence in his own fortunes. And yet, implicit in that silence he had kept, but unacknowledged in his own thoughts, had been the fear of her demeanour in the crisis. He knew her for a worldly woman, clad in great aspirations; he had taken the measure of her trivial vanities; he had sounded the shallows of her passionless heart; and still he had trusted, still he had nursed an empty faith in her affection. But now at this slight repulse somehow the props swayed beneath his rickety platform, and his thoughts ran in a darker current of despair. The bankruptcy, the guilt, the horror of his defalcations, were no longer the Evil to come, but merely now the steps by which he mounted to the real tragedy of his life.

Rosewarne quietly took up his hat, and drawing on his coat, passed out of the house and walked slowly towards the City.

It was upon two o'clock when Mrs. Rosewarne descended from the portico of her house and was enclosed within her landau by the footman. She was in a fervour which became her admirably; her cheeks were touched with points of colour, and her fine eyes brightened as with the flash of steel. She itched to try the temper of her diplomacy, and, as she entered the drawing-room of her hostess, the thought that she was well equipped for the encounter filled her anew with zest. Her eyes, piercing from that handsome face, challenged the luncheon-party. Mrs. Charters gave her a loud effusive welcome, as the beauty of the entertainment, and a general murmur of greeting seemed to salute her ears. Stepping a pace from the company and engaging easily with her hostess, Mrs. Rosewarne denoted the guests with sharp glances. Of her own disposition at the table she could have no certainty; the occasion was urgent; and with a nod she summoned Lord Hambleton to her side.

" And you, Lord Hambleton!" said she with a pretty air of surprise, " why, I heard you were in Scotland."

" Scotland ! " he said, shrugging his shoulders and smiling. " What ! Scotland in January, and the session like a drawn sword at one's heart."

" Ah ! " she replied, " I had forgotten the session. And yet my poor husband talks enough about it."

" Indeed ! " said the Whip with good-humour, " there is still some one, then, who bothers about us."

She lifted her shoulders slightly, as one who would disclaim a personal participation in the folly.

" Doesn't every one ? " she asked.

" Why, we talk of ourselves," said he laughing, " but I did not know any one else took an interest in us. We have outlived our time, you see. We are early Victorians, so to speak. Representative government is a glorious tradition, like the English flag or Balaclava—very brave, very wonderful, but very unimportant. I know we bulk largely in the newspapers. It is our *métier*. But I wonder why. The habit exists when the utility is fled. Is it because the advertisers love us, do you think? It is the only reason I can conceive. We all owe our being to the Births, Deaths, and Marriages. The servant-girl, my dear Mrs. Rosewarne, confers upon me the fame of a Tuesday's issue, for the shilling she expends upon a 'Wanted.' Alas!" He pulled his features into an expression of dismay. "When the hoarding and the sky-sign come in we shall go out."

Mrs. Rosewarne laughed gently, a demure intelligence shining from her eyes.

"And you," said he quizzically, "you don't care for us?"

"Oh, I!" she retorted with a sigh. "Yes, I talk of you. I am obliged to talk of you over the hearth-rug. I assure you I have all your names by rote, and rattle them off like a poll-parrot."

"Ah!" said Lord Hambleton, peering

into her face curiously; " I can appreciate your tone.   You are weary of us."

" Frankly, yes," said she, smiling.   They both laughed, and he made a gesture of apology.

" Why ? " he asked.

The voice of a butler cried from the doorway; there was a sudden stir in the room, and then a little hush.

" We are separated, alas! " said Lord Hambleton.

" Not at all," said Mrs. Charters, suddenly, at his elbows.   " I believe you are neighbours."

Mrs. Rosewarne's heart bounded in her side, and then beat placidly with its accustomed rhythm.   Lord Hambleton looked at her.   " That's very nice," he murmured.

At the table he turned to her with an immediate air of interest.   " Why ? " he repeated.

Her gaze had wandered across the table

with a profession of gentle indifference. She was surveying the guests with a remote abstraction; plucked out of which she glanced at him with a pretty hint of embarrassment, her forehead frowning as though to recover the topic of their conversation.

" Why ? " she echoed; and then: " Oh, yes," said she, smiling as out of a memory regained. " Because—well, because, what does it all avail ? "

· " Nothing, I grant you," he replied easily, " or very little, save to ourselves. You forget us. We have our business. Our fathers gamed and we talk. Don't forget us."

He spoke in railing tones, almost jocosely, and she lifted her eyebrows a line.

" Ah, yes ! " she assented. " Yes, but me and the rest of us, are we to keep you in your fun ? "

He paused before replying, and noted

every particular distinction in her handsome face. They were at close quarters;
he leaned a trifle nearer, and lowered his
voice to a mocking confidence:

" Mrs. Rosewarne, you would never blow
upon us, surely." He feigned to hang in
suspense upon her answer; the proximity
touched him with a queer elation; she shot
upon him one of her loveliest glances.

" I can hold my tongue for a friend, Lord
Hambleton."

" Come," he said, nodding, " that is better. That is a very sportsmanlike spirit."

Mrs. Rosewarne considered, smiling the
while she continued her meal. The approach was long, but to manœuvre height-
ened her spirits, and she was now to make
a bolder movement.

" But why," she asked, " should you expect mercy from a woman ?"

" I don't, Heaven knows," he responded
promptly; " I wonder at it, and admire."

"I think you have had a very long innings," said she, thoughtfully, "and were it in my power I would show no mercy."

Lord Hambleton laughed contentedly. "Oh, well!" he said.

"There is no opportunity for women," continued Mrs. Rosewarne, wistfully; "there has never been."

"Who would have suspected that you were ambitious?" commented Lord Hambleton, archly.

She threw up her jewelled fingers. "Ambitious!" she said, impatiently. "I am a woman. Where is the use? That is your business; mine is the boudoir, naturally. We are always—in the field, you call it, don't you? Men go to the wickets. My poor husband would tear out his heart for a seat. He is sound, he is good, he has wits, he is tolerable; he would serve excellently well upon a minor committee, and would never give a shadow of trouble. He would never ask questions, or soar at Cabinets. Yet it is, I suppose, ambition of a kind. But me! What has it to do with me! A woman knows nothing—of politics, no more than life. I can enjoy no vicarious pomp. No! give me the authority myself; give me a share in it, Lord Hambleton, and then I will tell you if I am ambitious!"

She put her head aside, and appeared with this tirade to drop the subject; she made a feint of listening to a conversation across the table. She smiled at the jest that reached her as if she had forgotten her companion. And yet she was aware that the aspect of her face, at which he was staring, was that which best became her. Lord Hambleton watched the long and delicate lines warm with soft blood, and his own senses were strangely affected.

"But you would influence him," he said presently. She came back with a display of reluctance, and seemed to pause, searching for his meaning.

"Oh!" she said, "Heavens! I have higher aims than that. Make him Under-Secretary, and he would be worth influencing; but poor Freddy——" She shrugged her shoulders and looked away again, as though impatient of the subject. Perhaps she was really tired of the conversation, he reflected.

"Well, here we are," he said, with deprecation in his voice, "talking all the time on a subject which you professed at the outset bored you. How unpardonable of me!"

"Bored me!" she said, opening her eyes at him and very innocently. "Oh, not talking with any one worth while."

Lord Hambleton's eyes dropped, and he was silent. The wine had fired his blood no less than her beauty. He looked up again, and met her glance by misadventure. A show of colour flooded her face; the pulses beat in her white throat. He did not know why, but his hands trembled a little, and a bar seemed broken down between them.

" Upon my soul!" he said, with an excited laugh, " I believe you would regenerate us all, if you were in the House!"

" I'm sure I should," she said gaily. Her heart fluttered in her side. " But there is no chance of that; I could only keep a *salon*. Why isn't it done? There is no Récamier nowadays; there is no Blessington. There is even no Whip's wife."

She was conscious of a faint shudder as she made this impudent stroke, and withdrew in a tremble into herself. She lay back in her chair, frightened. The words fell opportunely into Lord Hambleton's heart; he had no suspicion that they were deliberate, and the blood danced lightly along his arteries.

" You would hold a *salon* bravely," he said.

" Try me," she said with the affectation of playful laughter.

He laughed with her, and " Oh, we shall have everything out of you by-and-bye," said he. " We will bide our time. What we want just now more than anything is sound men. Now Mr. Rosewarne——"

" Poor Freddy is as sound as Big Ben, I suppose," said Mrs. Rosewarne, indifferently.

She felt the blood burning in her cheeks. Their eyes encountered. It seemed to him that they had a private secret together. He scarce knew what it was, so far had his sensations crowded upon his intelligence; but some connection, woven through the clatter of that public meal, held him and her in common. With her quick wit she was aware of his thought. She felt flushed with her own beauty. It was not of her husband he was thinking, and she was aware that he believed she too was not considering him.

The understanding lay between themselves. She rose triumphant; her heart spoke in loud acclamations.

"Ah, well," she said, with a tiny sigh, "I must wait, then, for old age to found my *salon*."

"No," he replied, smiling at her; "and why? We must have your husband in the House. Then you may begin at once."

"My husband!" she echoed, as though recalled to some vague and distasteful consideration.

"Yes. You must have this *salon*. It may save us."

She looked at him, as if in doubt. He rose beside her. He overtopped her by a head, and a certain strength about his forehead attracted her. Ah! If this had been her husband! The regret flashed and was gone.

"Come and tell him," she said suddenly.

He misinterpreted the fervour in her eyes.

' When ?'' he asked.

'' To-night,'' she murmured.

There was a momentary pause, and then,
'' To-night,'' he assented, taking her hand.

Mrs. Rosewarne moved easily within the
retinue of her admirers in the drawing-
room. She regarded the company with cool
eyes of triumph. She held their gazes; the
looks they passed upon her fed her complacency; she was sensible of her new distinction among them. And when, later,
she returned to her house, she was still
under the escort of success. The excitement ran like rich wine in her body, and
under its stimulus her pale face was flushed
with a tide of colour. She dressed for dinner, radiant, and crowned, as she conceived,
with incomparable splendour. The presid-
ing enthusiasm of her mind prevailed upon
her beauty. In the glass she considered
her looks, and smilingly softened the glory
of her cheeks. Her thoughts reverted with

amiable contempt to her husband, and in a measure he too was exalted in her own triumph. She descended the stairs, and swept into the dining-room in the full current of her happiness; and she had a sudden sense of repulse upon finding the room vacant.

" Where is your master ?" she asked of the servant, who stood in observant silence at the further end of the room.

Williams had seen him come in an hour ago; he had retired to his room. Should he go and inquire ?

" No: we will give him a few minutes," said she, seating herself.

She held communion with her own surprises. She anticipated his sensations; if he had failed with Maclagan, she, at least, had had better fortune, and for a moment Freddy and she were wrapt in common fellowship, set upon a common course. But as the time wore on, and he made no appearance, she grew restless and fidgeted; a little annoyance mingled with her good-humour; the warmth of her success ebbed away. She despatched Williams to bring the laggard down, and when he had returned with the report that he could get no answer, she picked up her skirts, and with lowering brows herself undertook the mission.

Mrs. Rosewarne paused outside her husband's room, and knocked. There was no response, and turning the handle of the door impatiently, she entered. The lamp burned low, and Freddy lay upon the bed, sprawling in an attitude of graceless comfort. The noise of his hard breathing sounded in the chamber, and the odour of strong spirit filled the air. In an access of angry disgust she shook him by the shoulders, and he lifted a stupid face to her, his eyes shot with blood.

" Is it you, Dolly ? " he asked thickly.

Her voice rose on a high note of anger.

' Do you know that the gong has gone

this half-hour? Bah! You have been drinking, you beast!"

He sat up, staring at her vacantly, and slowly his eyes grew quick with life and fury.

"And what the devil is it to you if I have?" he said savagely. "Why, in hell's name, don't you leave me alone? What are you doing here? What are you doing in my room? It was you relegated me to this. What are you doing here?"

"I came," said she coldly, "to call you to dinner; but since you have chosen to be the beast you are, I will leave you."

At the word, she swept upon her heel and was gone. Rosewarne sat for some minutes dully upon his bed. The flame of his anger had leapt and died, and he was now hunched up physically and morally, like a craven: his wits dispersed, his mind groping in a dreadful space for some palpable occasion of pain. Presently his reason flowed once more, and piece by piece he resumed the horrible round of life. Thereafter came a deep, warm gush of reason and affection. He had been brutal; he had been the beast she termed him. He had used her evilly when she meant but kindly by him. His heart wept for her and for himself—she was his love and his darling. He would go and pour forth his tears of regret upon her. She had naturally been struck to the heart to see him thus unmanned and sapped in the very foundations of his mind. She did not know. How could she ? . . . But he must tell her! The thought fetched him to a sudden term in the maudlin consideration of his streaming emotions. Drawn at this instant before the presence of that Terror, he trembled and rocked upon his couch. He threw the gathering thoughts aside. He must not suffer them to cloud his mind again. He must go forth and enter the room with the pleading face of a penitent. It was her due; it was his necessity—nay, this control was demanded by the very terms of his being.

He set his dress in order; he combed himself before the glass, and regarded his own grimacing image. " I will think of nothing," he murmured. " I am a man. There is nothing wrong. I can assume that for an hour. I shall go straight to Dolly. I must ward it all off. It will suffice later. Now! I am going to begin—Now! I will think of nothing. Do you hear, you fool! Oh, you damned, silly fool! You know it is fatal if you don't. Stop. No figures; no worries. Just thrust them aside. It can't matter that two and two make four when they ought to make five. Now then! From this moment I stop. I am a man," he explained to his grimacing image. " No more figures. I will begin. No worries! Now!" He pulled out his watch. " In five seconds I will start." He saw the hand jump round.

"Now!" and then in the ear of his brain a thin voice cried, softly insistent: "Five thousand and that odd two hundred. Is that all right? Go back on it. Give them just a glance." He paused, but the blood in his head stood still. At the cross-ways he trembled, dazed with the conflict of the two desires. "Well, one glance."

At that the whole body of his madness rolled back upon him through the rift. He threw up his hands, and, hiding his face in the bed-clothes, groaned. "Now!" he said again, flinging himself peremptorily to his feet. He straightened his figure. "Now!" As if with a wild, reckless motion, he pulled to the door of his mind, and shutting his eyes, marched out of the room, laughing mechanically. "Dorothy, Dorothy, Dorothy!" he muttered under his breath.

Rosewarne entered the dining-room with a quick tread and a moving galvanic smile.

"Dolly, forgive me," he said; "I am

late. Where are you ? Oh, Williams, some fish. That will do.''

He started to talk in a very hurried manner, but with humble cheerfulness. His wife stared at him coldly, answering in short, colourless sentences. But he made amends for her reticence with a continuous stream of talk. He chattered freely, and he ate ravenously. He rambled on through numberless topics with no apparent connection. All the reserves of his nature were enrolled in that gallant essay to fence him from the Horror of his life, and hedge him safely about with casual trifles. Of a sudden he saw things clear about him. A certain bright wit shone in his soliloquies; he spoke with that incoherence and irresponsibility which begets sometimes effective phrasing. His wife considered him; the novelty of his conversation struck her, its frivolity took her with admiration. Slowly the barriers of her own reserve broke down, the sense of satisfaction in herself grew upon her, and by degrees her good-humour returned. She joined in his talk, laughed a little, was inspired by his mood into newer, fresher, wilder hopes. No word was said about the scene in the bedroom; it had dropped into past history, and their feet were set to the future. And when Williams was gone, she turned swiftly upon him, her zeal showing in her eyes.

"And now, Freddy," she said, "tell me all about Maclagan."

His face started into haggard lines; he lowered his eyes, and, with a short laugh, shook his head.

"Later; not now," he said. "You begin."

She laughed also. "I have seen Lord Hambleton," she said, with a burst of excitement. "He is coming to-night." And watched upon his face for the effect.

"Oh, you clever girl!" he cried, his eyes

smiling, his lips quivering slightly. "You clever girl."

Again she laughed. It almost seemed to her at that moment that she loved him.

"Ah, you would think so, if you knew how I managed it."

"But I know it, I know it," he cried, seizing her hand across the table. "You are as clever as you are beautiful."

He hardly recalled the point to which their conversation related; he was aware only of her proximity and her kindly eyes. She returned the pressure of his fingers faintly, and looked at him thoughtfully.

"You look tired, Freddy," she said. "I'm afraid you've had a very wearisome day."

"Yes," he assented with a tiny laugh. "I have had a bad day."

"Tell me," she said abruptly, "what about Maclagan?"

He rose. "Come into the study, then,"

he said in another voice. " I can tell you better there."

She followed him, laying a hand lightly upon his shoulder. She took her seat within the comfortable armchair, stretching herself out, with her feet to the fire and the red light upon her face and bosom. Rosewarne leaned his elbow on the mantel-piece.

" Well ? " she asked presently in a tone of invitation.

He started. " Dolly," he said slowly, "supposing I were—to die—would you——"

" Good gracious, Freddy, don't talk non-sense," she interrupted on his halting phrases. " We haven't come to talk about foolish things like that."

He made no answer, but stared harder into the fire. A sense of irritation grew upon Mrs. Rosewarne. Had he failed in his mission ? If he had, at least she had succeeded in hers, and the thought consoled her.

" Now, let me hear all about it.   Do be quick," she said.

He turned to her suddenly.   " Dolly, you must answer me; please answer me," he cried in agitation.   " You could not bear my death, could you ?   Say you couldn't."

" Of course not," she replied sharply.   " Why in the name of all that is decent will you harp on that ?   Don't be morbid."

" It will have to come to that," he said brokenly.

" Pooh !   Don't be foolish," she retorted. She regarded him critically.   Even in the red light the colour of his face, which had fallen into ugly lines, repelled her.   " Come, what is it ?   Is anything the matter with you ?   Have you seen your doctor ?   What are you keeping from me ? "

The questions ran off her tongue sharply, even acrimoniously.   She had anew the sense of irritation that he had chosen this hour to be ill.

"No," he replied in a blank voice, "I suppose I'm all right. I don't know. I've been—yes—I'm ill with the horrible trouble. I'm——" He fell quickly upon his knees, burying his face in her gown. "Oh, Dolly, Dolly," he sobbed, "I have ruined you, and you don't know it. It is all over—all over."

Her eyes opened in alarm, but she did not move. "What nonsense are you talking, Freddy?" she asked in an uncertain voice which rang harshly. "You're ill. You've been overworking. You mustn't. What foolishness!"

She laughed faintly, with embarrassment, and almost mechanically put out a hand and touched his hair as though vaguely to reassure him of his mistake; while all the time her heart thumped on and her mind was wondering in a daze.

At her touch he raised his head, and clutched her, crying, "Ah, you do love me, Dolly. You do love me. I knew

you loved me.   I knew you would be sorry
for me."

She sat motionless, fear reaching out arms
for her heart.   Slowly she was beginning to
understand.

"What is it that you have done?" she
asked in a dry voice.

He pressed her hand tightly, crushing her
fingers.   "I have taken money," he whispered, "trust money.   I am ruined.   I
must go to prison, unless I——"

She moistened her lips, impassive as ever.

"But you do love me," he repeated,
clinging to her.   "Yes, you do love me,
Dolly.   Even if I have to do—that thing,
you love me still."

Through all her being ran a repulsion
for this creature at her knees, but she was
clogged with her emotions and sat silent.

"Dolly, Dolly," he cried pathetically.
"I shall have to do it.   I know I shall have
to do it—I——" He looked up, gulping

down his sobs, as though seeking in her face for a contradiction. He knew the warm tears would fall upon him. Through his blurred vision he saw her mutely, indistinctly, raise her arms, extracting her hand from his grasp. He felt—he knew—he hoped—— Ah, she would throw them about his neck and draw him close in a passionate, pitiful embrace.

"Dolly, Dolly," he whispered, "I shall have to die."

With a rough movement she thrust him from her and got upon her feet.

"Die!" she exclaimed in a voice full of ineffable bitterness. "Die! Oh, my God, yes. That is the least you can do."

He lay where he had fallen to her push, huddled in a shapeless heap, stirring faintly. It was to her eyes as if some vermin upon which she had set her foot still moved with life. There was left in him no power of thought, no capacity of emotion. He was dimly conscious of misery, and he knew that she was standing by. Far away a tune sounded, and reverberated in his ears; it was the singing of the empty air. She was staring upon him with disgust and terror.

"Poor worm!" she said, in tense, low tones; and then her eyes alighted on her heaving bosom and the glories of her gown. The revulsion struck her like a blow, and she reeled under it. "You devil!" she cried. "You have ruined my life."

The sound of those sharp words smote upon his brain, and whipped his ragged soul. He rose suddenly to his feet, his face blazing with fury.

"Damn you," he cried passionately. "I have loved you. I have sold my soul for you. I have ruined my mind for you. Damn you, Dorothy. And you have no words for me. Damn you."

His voice trailed away into a tremulous sob, and he stood contemplating her with fixed eyes. She laughed hardly, withdrawing her skirts from his vicinity. His gaze wandered from her, and went furtively towards the mantelpiece. She followed it, and saw a revolver lying upon the marble.

"Bah!" she said. "You have not the courage."

At that moment a knock fell upon the door; after a pause she moved and opened it.

"Lord Hambleton, ma'am," said Williams. "He is in the drawing-room."

Breathing hard, she looked round at her husband. Rosewarne's dull eyes were fixed upon her. They interceded with her; they fawned upon her.

"I will be there in a moment," she said clearly. Rosewarne moved slowly to the table and sat down, resting his head in his hands. He made no protest; if he realised anything now, he realised that he had expected this. The door shut to behind her; a dull pain started in the base of his brain;

into the redoubts of his soul streamed swiftly the forces of sheer panic.

Mrs. Rosewarne entered the drawing-room, the tail of her dress rustling over the carpet. Lord Hambleton turned with this sound in his ears stirring him pleasantly.

"Well," said he, smiling, "you see I've come."

She gave him her hand and paused, confronting him. Her heart thumped like a hammer upon her side; her face was flushed with colour, and her lips quivered.

"It is good of you," she said tremulously; "won't you sit down?"

He did not heed her invitation, but shot a shrewd glance at her. Her voice startled him; the discomposure of her appearance arrested his eyes. He wondered what had happened. It could not be that his visit was the cause of this confusion. And yet he noted it with a thrill of satisfaction, such as he had experienced in the colloquy at Mrs. Charters's.

"You are very good to look at like this," he allowed himself to say. He picked up the thread of their communion where it had been dropped earlier that day. She was marvellously handsome; he had never admired a woman so much since his youth. The faint light spreading from the lamps illumined her brilliant face and threw up her figure in a kind of twilight against the wall.

Her heart palpitated audibly; it seemed to her that she had a sudden unreasonable desire to laugh. The squalid gloom of that chamber beyond lifted; it seemed remote and accidental. She was here with the comfortable eyes of this man upon her, contemplating her with admiration. She was not a parcel of that tragedy outside. She smiled broadly.

"Why, the better for my *salon*," she said.

What had excited her ? he asked himself.
" Ah ! we will arrange all that," he answered
with a familiar nod.

" You will ? " she asked eagerly—breathlessly.

" Why, certainly," he replied. " I
think we can manage it—between us."

She laughed aloud this time. " Yes, both
of us together," she said.

He met her eyes. Was it wine ? he
asked. Or was it——? Lord Hambleton's
body tingled with sensation. He had not
suspected that matters had progressed so
intimately between them. Almost involuntarily he put out a hand towards her. She
laughed awkwardly, and he drew it back.

" You should have had it long ago," he
said. " You have thrown away a chance."

" My life, you mean," she cried, breaking
in upon his mellifluous tones with a harsher
note.

She shifted her head towards the door as

if listening for a sound. Her action struck him for the moment as ungainly.

"Things do not always fall out as we want them," he said slowly.

"Not as you want them?" she asked, coming back to regard him. "Why, what more do you want?"

He watched her from his quiet eyes, which suddenly lost their equable expression. To him she had always appeared a woman of dispassion, but now the seeming surrender in her mind, the revolution in her character, flashed upon him with an extreme sense of emotion. His heart beat faster.

"I think you know," he said softly, and reaching forth, took her hand.

Swiftly she turned; a look of dread rushed into her eyes. All on a sudden the transactions of that neighbouring room leapt into proximity. She saw Freddy handling the revolver; she watched him lean over the table and cock it in the light; she saw him—— She gave a cry, and moved a step towards the door, with a frightened face.

"What is it?" asked Lord Hambleton in alarm. "You are ill. You——" She made no answer, and he seized her hand again. "Let me ring for a glass of wine," he whispered.

Mrs. Rosewarne laughed loudly in his face.

"No, no," she said; "it is nothing. Pray, don't. I shall be better."

She looked at him, and then turned her ear to the door again, listening with a white face. He watched her anxiously, but in his own mind the reason of her perturbation was clear. The thought was sweet to him.

"Well," said he; "and now to business."

"Business!" she echoed, and moved quickly to him, "I—— Please, you must excuse me, Lord Hambleton. My husband is ill. Do you mind? I——"

He rose abruptly. "I am very sorry,"

he said; " I will not trouble you, then, just now."

He took his hat. She had turned away and was hearkening with all her senses for that report that did not come. He bit his lips. Perhaps she had been overstrained. He could scarce say what feeling ran uppermost in his mind. She hurried him to the door, accompanying him herself.

" Must you go ? " she asked, stupidly, on the doorstep.

He looked at her; perhaps she really was ill. But she was very beautiful. She did not hear his answer. The rough wind blew through the open door and scattered her hair and her skirts. Lord Hambleton went down the steps. She watched him go. At that moment, somehow, a great revulsion overwhelmed her. She had listened, and there had been no discharge. What a fool she had been ! Of course, he had no courage. She had the desire to rush after Lord

Hambleton and call him back. She had tortured herself idly; she had played a silly part in a melodrama. She recalled Lord Hambleton's ardent gaze. There was a man! Ah, if this thing were not fastened about her neck! She stole back along the hall—furious. Once more she was confronted with the squalor of her position. Her indignation rose higher; she could see that pitiful creature crying for mercy, crying for affection. Bah! He was too cowardly to die. Burning with the old anger, she crossed to the study and opened the door. She would have it out with him; they should understand their position. With Lord Hambleton the dignified prospects of her life had vanished, and she was flung back upon a mean and ignominious lot.

Rosewarne was seated in the armchair; the revolver rested where it had lain upon the mantelpiece. He made no movement to rise as she returned, and she stood for a second looking down upon him from behind with curling lips. A bottle of whisky and a glass stood upon the table at his elbow. It was probable that he had drunk himself to sleep.

"Are you awake?" she called sharply. He made no sign. She bent over angrily and shook him.

His head fell to her touch, and from his fingers a little phial tumbled upon the floor.

III

The Stone Chamber

IT was not until early summer that Warrington took possession of Marvyn Abbey.
He had bought the property in the preceding autumn, but the place had so fallen into
decay through the disorders of time that
more than six months elapsed ere it was
inhabitable. The delay, however, fell out
conveniently for Warrington; for the Bosanquets spent the winter abroad, and nothing
must suit but he must spend it with them.
There was never a man who pursued his
passion with such ardour. He was ever at
Miss Bosanquet's skirts, and bade fair to
make her as steadfast a husband as he was
attached a lover. Thus it was not until

after his return from that prolonged exile
that he had the opportunity of inspecting
the repairs discharged by his architect. He
was nothing out of the common in character, but was full of kindly impulses and a
fellow of impetuous blood. When he called
upon me in my chambers he spoke with
some excitement of his Abbey, as also of
his approaching marriage; and finally, breaking into an exhibition of genuine affection,
declared that we had been so long and so
continuously intimate that I, and none
other, must help him warm his house and
marry his bride. It had indeed been
always understood between us that I should
serve him at the ceremony, but now it
appeared that I must start my duties even
earlier. The prospect of a summer holiday
in Utterbourne pleased me. It was a
charming village, set upon the slope of a
wooded hill and within call of the sea. I
had a slight knowledge of the district from

a riding excursion taken through that part of Devonshire; and years before, and ere Warrington had come into his money, had viewed the Abbey ruins from a distance with the polite curiosity of a passing tourist.

I examined them now with new eyes as we drove up the avenue. The face which the ancient building presented to the valley was of magnificent design, but now much worn and battered. Part of it, the·right wing, I judged to be long past the uses of a dwelling, for the walls had crumbled away, huge gaps opened in the foundations, and the roof was quite dismantled. Warrington had very wisely left this portion to its own sinister decay; it was the left wing which had been restored, and which we were to inhabit. The entrance, I will confess, was a little mean, for the large doorway had been bricked up and an ordinary modern door gave upon the spacious terrace and the winding gardens. But apart from this, the work of restoration had been undertaken with skill and piety, and the interior had retained its native dignity, while resuming an air of proper comfort. The old oak had been repaired congruous with the original designs, and the great rooms had been as little altered as was requisite to adapt them for daily use.

Warrington passed quickly from chamber to chamber in evident delight, directing my attention upon this and upon that, and eagerly requiring my congratulations and approval. My comments must have satisfied him, for the place attracted me vastly. The only criticism I ventured was to remark upon the size of the rooms and to question if they might not dwarf the insignificant human figures they were to entertain.

He laughed. "Not a bit," said he. "Roaring fires in winter in those fine old fireplaces; and as for summer, the more space the better. We shall be jolly."

I followed him along the noble hall, and we stopped before a small door of very black oak.

"The bedrooms," he explained, as he turned the key, "are all upstairs, but mine is not ready yet. And besides, I am reserving it; I won't sleep in it till—you understand," he concluded, with a smiling suggestion of embarrassment.

I understood very well. He threw the door open.

"I am going to use this in the meantime," he continued. "Queer little room, isn't it? It used to be a sort of library. How do you think it looks?"

We had entered as he spoke, and stood, distributing our glances in that vague and general way in which a room is surveyed. It was a chamber of much smaller proportions than the rest, and was dimly lighted by two long narrow windows sunk in the great walls. The bed and the modern fittings looked strangely out of keeping with its ancient privacy. The walls were rudely distempered with barbaric frescos, dating, I conjectured, from the fourteenth century; and the floor was of stone, worn into grooves and hollows with the feet of many generations. As I was taking in these facts, there came over me a sudden curiosity as to those dead Marvyns who had held the Abbey for so long. This silent chamber seemed to suggest questions of their history; it spoke eloquently of past ages and past deeds, fallen now into oblivion. Here, within these thick walls, no echo from the outer world might carry, no sound would ring within its solitary seclusion. Even the silence seemed to confer with one upon the ancient transactions of that extinct House.

Warrington stirred, and turned suddenly to me. " I hope it's not damp," said he, with a slight shiver. " It looks rather solemn. I thought furniture would brighten it up."

"I should think it would be very comfortable," said I. "You will never be disturbed by any sounds at any rate."

"No," he answered, hesitatingly; and then, quickly, on one of his impulses: "Hang it, Heywood, there's too much silence here for me." Then he laughed. "Oh, I shall do very well for a month or two." And with that appeared to return to his former placid cheerfulness.

The train of thought started in that sombre chamber served to entertain me several times that day. I questioned Warrington at dinner, which we took in one of the smaller rooms, commanding a lovely prospect of dale and sea. He shook his head. Archæological lore, as indeed anything else out of the borders of actual life, held very little interest for him.

"The Marvyns died out in 1714, I believe," he said, indifferently; "someone told me that—the man I bought it from, I think. They might just as well have kept the place up since; but I think it has been only occupied twice between then and now, and the last time was forty years ago. It would have rotted to pieces if I hadn't taken it. Perhaps Mrs. Batty could tell you. She's lived in these parts almost all her life."

To humour me, and affected, I doubt not, by a certain pride in his new possession, he put the query to his housekeeper upon her appearance subsequently; but it seemed that her knowledge was little fuller than his own, though she had gathered some vague traditions of the countryside. The Marvyns had not left a reputable name, if rumour spoke truly; theirs was a family to which black deeds had been credited. They were ill-starred also in their fortunes, and had become extinct suddenly; but for the rest, the events had fallen too many generations ago to be current now between the memories of the village.

Warrington, who was more eager to discuss the future than to recall the past, was vastly excited by his anticipations. St. Pharamond, Sir William Bosanquet's house, lay across the valley, barely five miles away; and as the family had now returned, it was easy to forgive Warrington's elation.

" What do you think ? " he said, late that evening; and clapping me upon the shoulder, " You have seen Marion; here is the house. Am I not lucky ? Damn it, Heywood, I'm not pious, but I am disposed to thank God! I'm not a bad fellow, but I'm no saint; it's fortunate that it's not only the virtuous that are rewarded. In fact, it's usually contrariwise. I owe this to—Lord, I don't know what I owe it to. Is it my money ? Of course, Marion doesn't care a rap for that; but then, you see, I mightn't have known her without it. Of course, there's the house, too. I'm thankful I have money. At any rate, here's my new life.

Just look about and take it in, old fellow. If you knew how a man may be ashamed of himself! But there, I've done. You know I'm decent at heart—you must count my life from to-day.'' And with this outbreak he lifted the glass between fingers that trembled with the warmth of his emotions, and tossed off his wine.

He did himself but justice when he claimed to be a good fellow; and, in truth, I was myself somewhat moved by his obvious feeling. I remember that we shook hands very affectionately, and my sympathy was the prelude to a long and confidential talk, which lasted until quite a late hour.

At the foot of the staircase, where we parted, he detained me.

'' This is the last of my wayward days,'' he said, with a smile. '' Late hours—liquor —all go. You shall see. Good-night. You know your room. I shall be up long before you.'' And with that he vanished briskly into the darkness that hung about the lower parts of the passage.

I watched him go, and it struck me quite vaguely what a slight impression his candle made upon that channel of opaque gloom. It seemed merely as a thread of light that illumined nothing. Warrington himself was rapt into the prevalent blackness; but long afterwards, and even when his footsteps had died away upon the heavy carpet, the tiny beam was visible, advancing and flickering in the distance.

My window, which was modern, opened upon a little balcony, where, as the night was warm and I was indisposed for sleep, I spent half an hour enjoying the air. I was in a sentimental mood, and my thoughts turned upon the suggestions which Warrington's conversation had induced. It was not until I was in bed, and had blown out the light, that they settled upon the square, dark chamber in which my host was to pass the night. As I have said, I was wakeful, owing, no doubt, to the high pitch of the emotions which we had encouraged; but presently my fancies became inarticulate and incoherent, and then I was overtaken by profound sleep.

Warrington was up before me, as he had predicted, and met me in the breakfast-room.

"What a beggar you are to sleep!" he said, with a smile. "I've hammered at your door for half an hour."

I apologised for myself, alleging the rich country air in my defence, and mentioned that I had had some difficulty in getting to sleep.

"So had I," he remarked, as we sat down to the table. "We got very excited, I suppose. Just see what you have there, Heywood. Eggs? Oh, damn it, one can have too much of eggs!" He frowned, and lifted a third cover. "Why in the name of common sense can't Mrs. Batty give us more variety ?" he asked, impatiently.

I deprecated his displeasure, suggesting that we should do very well; indeed, his discontent seemed to me quite unnecessary. But I supposed Warrington had been rather spoiled by many years of club life.

He settled himself without replying, and began to pick over his plate in a gingerly manner.

" There's one thing I will have here, Heywood," he observed. " I will have things well appointed. I'm not going to let life in the country mean an uncomfortable life. A man can't change the habits of a lifetime."

In contrast with his exhilarated professions of the previous evening, this struck me with a sense of amusement at the moment; and the incongruity may have occurred to him, for he went on: " Marion's not over strong, you know, and must have things *comme il faut*. She shan't decline upon a lower level. The worst of these rustics is that they have no imagination.'' He held up a piece of bacon on his fork, and surveyed it with disgust. '' Now, look at that! Why the devil don't they take tips from civilised people like the French ?''

It was so unlike him to exhibit this petulance that I put it down to a bad night, and without discovering the connection of my thoughts, asked him how he liked his bedroom.

'' Oh, pretty well, pretty well,'' he said, indifferently. '' It's not so cold as I thought. But I slept badly. I always do in a strange bed ''; and pushing aside his plate, he lit a cigarette. '' When you've finished that garbage, Heywood, we'll have a stroll round the Abbey,'' he said.

His good temper returned during our walk, and he indicated to me various improvements which he contemplated, with something of his old ardour. The left wing of the house, as I have said, was entire, but a little apart were the ruins of a chapel. Surrounded by a low moss-grown wall, it was full of picturesque charm; the roofless chancel was spread with ivy, but the aisles were intact. Grass grew between the stones and the floor, and many creepers had strayed through chinks in the wall into those sacred precincts. The solemn quietude of the ruin, maintained under the spell of death, awed me a little, but upon Warrington apparently it made no impression. He was only zealous that I should properly appreciate the distinction of such a property. I stooped and drew the weeds away from one of the slabs in the aisle, and was able to trace upon it the relics of lettering, well-nigh obliterated under the corrosion of time.

"There are tombs," said I.

"Oh, yes," he answered, with a certain relish. "I understand the Marvyns used it as a mausoleum. They are all buried here. Some good brasses, I am told."

The associations of the place engaged me; the aspect of the Abbey faced the past; it seemed to refuse communion with the present; and somehow the thought of those two decent humdrum lives which should be spent within its shelter savoured of the incongruous. The white-capped maids and the emblazoned butlers that should tread these halls offered a ridiculous appearance beside my fancies of the ancient building. For all that, I envied Warrington his home, and so I told him, with a humorous hint that I was fitter to appreciate its glories than himself.

He laughed. " Oh, I don't know," said he. " I like the old-world look as much as you do. I have always had a notion of something venerable. It seems to serve you for ancestors." And he was undoubtedly delighted with my enthusiasm.

But at lunch again he chopped round to his previous irritation, only now quite another matter provoked his anger. He had received a letter by the second post from Miss Bosanquet, which, if I may judge from his perplexity, must have been unusually confused. He read and re-read it, his brow lowering.

"What the deuce does she mean?" he asked, testily. "She first makes an arrangement for us to ride over to-day, and now I can't make out whether we are to go to St. Pharamond, or they are coming to us. Just look at it, will you, Heywood?"

I glanced through the note, but could offer no final solution, whereupon he broke out again:

"That's just like women—they never can say anything straightforwardly. Why, in the name of goodness, couldn't she leave things as they were? You see," he observed, rather in answer, as I fancied, to my silence, " we don't know what to do now; if we stay here they mayn't come, and if we go probably we shall cross them." And he snapped his fingers in annoyance.

I was cheerful enough, perhaps because the responsibility was not mine, and ventured to suggest that we might ride over, and return if we missed them. But he dismissed the subject sharply by saying:

" No, I'll stay. I'm not going on a fool's errand," and drew my attention to some point in the decoration of the room.

The Bosanquets did not arrive during the afternoon, and Warrington's ill-humour increased. His love-sick state pleaded in excuse of him, but he was certainly not a pleasant companion. He was sour and snappish, and one could introduce no statement to which he would not find a contradiction. So unamiable did he grow that at last I discovered a pretext to leave him, and rambled to the back of the Abbey into the precincts of the old chapel. The day was falling, and the summer sun flared through the western windows upon the bare aisle. The creepers rustled upon the gaping walls, and the tall grasses waved in shadows over the bodies of the forgotten dead. As I stood contemplating the effect, and meditating greatly upon the anterior fortunes of the Abbey, my attention fell upon a huge slab of marble, upon which the yellow light struck sharply. The faded lettering rose into greater definition before my eyes and I read slowly:

"*Here lyeth the body of Sir Rupert Marvyn.*"

Beyond a date, very difficult to decipher, there was nothing more; of eulogy, of style, of record, of pious considerations such as were usual to the period, not a word. I read the numerals variously as 1723 and 1745; but however they ran it was probable that the stone covered the resting-place of the last Marvyn. The history of this futile house interested me not a little, partly for Warrington's sake, and in part from a natural bent towards ancient records; and I made a mental note of the name and date.

When I returned Warrington's surliness had entirely vanished, and had given place to an effusion of boisterous spirits. He apologised jovially for his bad temper.

"It was the disappointment of not seeing Marion," he said. "You will understand that some day, old fellow. But, anyhow, we'll go over to-morrow"; and forthwith proceeded to enliven the dinner with an ostentation of good-fellowship I had seldom witnessed in him. I began to suspect that he had heard again from St. Pharamond, though he chose to conceal the fact from me. The wine was admirable; though Warrington himself was no great judge, he had entrusted the selection to a good palate. We had a merry meal, drank a little more than was prudent, and smoked our cigars upon the terrace in the fresh air. Warrington was restless. He pushed his glass from him. "I'll tell you what, old chap," he broke out, "I'll give you a game of billiards. I've got a decent table."

I demurred. The air was too delicious, and I was in no humour for a sharp use of my wits. He laughed, though he seemed rather disappointed.

"It's almost sacrilege to play billiards in an Abbey," I said, whimsically. "What would the ghosts of the old Marvyns think?"

"Oh, hang the Marvyns!" he rejoined, crossly. "You're always talking of them."

He rose and entered the house, returning presently with a flagon of whiskey and some glasses.

"Try this," he said. "We've had no liqueurs"; and pouring out some spirit he swallowed it raw.

I stared, for Warrington rarely took spirits, being more of a wine drinker; moreover, he must have taken nearly the quarter of a tumbler. But he did not notice my surprise, and, seating himself, lit another cigar.

" I don't mean to have things quiet here," he observed, reflectively. " I don't believe in your stagnant rustic life. What I intend to do is to keep the place warm—plenty of house parties, things going on all the year. I shall expect you down for the shooting, Ned. The coverts promise well this year."

I assented willingly enough, and he rambled on again.

" I don't know that I shall use the Abbey so much. I think I'll live in town a good deal. It's brighter there. I don't know though. I like the place. Hang it, it's a rattling good shop, there's no mistake about it. Look here," he broke off, abruptly, " bring your glass in, and I'll show you something."

I was little inclined to move, but he was so peremptory that I followed him with a sigh. We entered one of the smaller rooms which overlooked the terrace, and had been diverted into a comfortable library. He flung back the windows.

"There's air for you," he cried. "Now, sit down," and walking to a cupboard produced a second flagon of whiskey. "Irish!" he ejaculated, clumping it on the table. "Take your choice," and turning again to the cupboard, presently sat down with his hands under the table. "Now, then, Ned," he said, with a short laugh. "Fill up, and we'll have some fun," with which he suddenly threw a pack of cards upon the board.

I opened my eyes, for I do not suppose Warrington had touched cards since his college days; but, interpreting my look in his own way, he cried:

"Oh, I'm not married yet. Warrington's his own man still. Poker? Eh?"

"Anything you like," said I, with resignation.

A peculiar expression of delight gleamed in his eyes, and he shuffled the cards feverishly.

"Cut," said he, and helped himself to more whiskey.

It was shameful to be playing there with that beautiful night without, but there seemed no help for it. Warrington had a run of luck, though he played with little skill; and his excitement grew as he won.

"Let us make it ten shillings," he suggested.

I shook my head. "You forget I'm not a millionaire," I replied.

"Bah!" he cried. "I like a game worth the victory. Well, fire away."

His eyes gloated upon the cards, and he fingered them with unctuous affection. The behaviour of the man amazed me. I began to win.

Warrington's face slowly assumed a dull, lowering expression; he played eagerly, avariciously; he disputed my points, and was querulous.

"Oh, we've had enough!" I cried in distaste.

"By Jove, you don't!" he exclaimed, jumping to his feet. "You're the winner, Heywood, and I'll see you damned before I let you off my revenge!"

The words startled me no less than the fury which rang in his accents. I gazed at him in stupefaction. The whites of his eyes showed wildly, and a sullen, angry look determined his face. Suddenly I was arrested by the suspicion of something upon his neck.

"What's that?" I asked. "You've cut yourself."

He put his hand to his face. "Non-sense," he replied, in a surly fashion.

I looked closer, and then I saw my mistake. It was a round, faint red mark, the size of a florin, upon the column of his throat, and I set it down to the accidental pressure of some button.

" Come on ! " he insisted, impatiently.

" Bah ! Warrington," I said, for I imagined that he had been over-excited by the whiskey he had taken. " It's only a matter of a few pounds. Why make a fuss ? To-morrow will serve."

After a moment his eyes fell, and he gave an awkward laugh. " Oh, well, that'll do," said he. " But I got so infernally excited."

" Whiskey," said I, sententiously.

He glanced at the bottle. " How many glasses have I had ? " and he whistled. " By Jove, Ned, this won't do! I must turn over a new leaf. Come on; let's look at the night."

I was only too glad to get away from the table, and we were soon upon the terrace again. Warrington was silent, and his gaze

went constantly across the valley, where the
moon was rising, and in the direction in
which, as he had indicated to me, St. Pharamond lay.   When he said good-night he
was still pre-occupied.

" I hope you will sleep better," he said.

" And you, too," I added.

He smiled.   " I don't suppose I shall
wake the whole night through," he said;
and then, as I was turning to go, he caught
me quickly by the arm.

" Ned," he said, impulsively and very
earnestly, " don't let me make a fool of
myself again.   I know it's the excitement
of everything.   But I want to be as good
as I can for her."

I pressed his hand.   " All right, old fellow," I said; and we parted.

I think I have never enjoyed sounder
slumber than that night.   The first thing I
was aware of was the singing of thrushes
outside my window.   I rose and looked

forth, and the sun was hanging high in the eastern sky, the grass and the young green of the trees were shining with dew. With an uncomfortable feeling that I was very late I hastily dressed and went downstairs. Warrington was waiting for me in the breakfast-room, as upon the previous morning, and when he turned from the window at my approach, the sight of his face startled me. It was drawn and haggard, and his eyes were shot with blood; it was a face broken and savage with dissipation. He made no answer to my questioning, but seated himself with a morose air.

"Now you have come," he said, sullenly, "we may as well begin. But it's not my fault if the coffee's cold."

I examined him critically, and passed some comment upon his appearance.

"You don't look up to much," I said. "Another bad night?"

"No; I slept well enough," he responded,

ungraciously; and then, after a pause: " I'll tell you what, Heywood. You shall give me my revenge after breakfast."

" Nonsense," I said, after a momentary silence. " You're going over to St. Pharamond."

" Hang it!" was his retort, " one can't be always bothering about women. You seem mightily indisposed to meet me again."

" I certainly won't this morning," I answered, rather sharply, for the man's manner grated upon me. " This evening, if you like; and then the silly business shall end."

He said something in an undertone of grumble, and the rest of the meal passed in silence. But I entertained an uneasy suspicion of him, and after all he was my friend, with whom I was under obligations not to quarrel; and so when we rose, I approached him.

" Look here, Warrington," I said. " What's the matter with you ? Have you been drinking ? Remember what you asked me last night."

" Hold your damned row!" was all the answer he vouchsafed, as he whirled away from me, but with an embarrassed display of shame.

But I was not to be put off in that way, and I spoke somewhat more sharply.

" We're going to have this out, Warrington," I said. " If you are ill, let us understand that; but I'm not going to stay here with you in this cantankerous spirit."

" I'm not ill," he replied testily.

" Look at yourself," I cried, and turned him about to the mirror over the mantelpiece.

He started a little, and a frown of perplexity gathered on his forehead.

" Good Lord! I'm not like that, Ned," he said, in a different voice. " I must have been drunk last night." And with a sort of groan, he directed a piteous look at me.

"Come," I was constrained to answer, "pull yourself together. The ride will do you good. And no more whisky."

"No, by Heaven, no!" he cried vehemently, and seemed to shiver; but then, suddenly taking my arm, he walked out of the room.

The morning lay still and golden. Warrington's eyes went forth across the valley.

"Come round to the stables, Ned," he said, impulsively. "You shall choose your own nag."

I shook my head. "I'll choose yours," said I, "but I am not going with you." He looked surprised. "No, ride by yourself. You don't want a companion on such an errand. I'll stay here, and pursue my investigations into the Marvyns."

A scowl crossed his face, but only for an instant, and then he answered: "All right, old chap; do as you like. Anyway, I'm off at once." And presently, when his horse was brought, he was laughing merrily.

"You'll have a dull day, Ned; but it's your own fault, you duffer. You'll have to lunch by yourself, as I shan't be back till late." And, gaily flourishing his whip, he trotted down the drive.

It was some relief to me to be rid of him, for, in truth, his moods had worn my nerves, and I had not looked for a holiday of this disquieting nature. When he returned, I had no doubt it would be with quite another face, and meanwhile I was excellent company for myself. After lunch I amused myself for half an hour with idle tricks upon the billiard-table, and, tiring of my pastime, fell upon the housekeeper as I returned along the corridor. She was a woman nearer to sixty than fifty, of a comfortable, portly figure, and an amiable expression. Her eyes invited me ever so respectfully to conversation, and stopping, I entered into talk. She inquired if I liked my room and how I slept.

" 'Tis a nice look-out you have, Sir," said she. " That was where old Lady Martin slept."

It appeared that she had served as kitchen-maid to the previous tenants of the Abbey, nearly fifty years before.

" Oh, I know the old house in and out," she asserted; " and I arranged the rooms with Mr. Warrington."

We were standing opposite the low doorway which gave entrance to Warrington's bedroom, and my eyes unconsciously shot in that direction. Mrs. Batty followed my glance.

" I didn't want him to have that," she said; " but he was set upon it. It's smallish for a bedroom, and in my opinion isn't fit for more than a lumber-room. That's what Sir William used it for."

I pushed open the door and stepped over the threshold, and the housekeeper followed me.

"No," she said, glancing round; "and it's in my mind that it's damp, Sir."

Again I had a curious feeling that the silence was speaking in my ear; the atmosphere was thick and heavy, and a musty smell, as of faded draperies, penetrated my nostrils. The whole room looked indescribably dingy, despite the new hangings. I went over to the narrow window and peered through the diamond panes. Outside, but seen dimly through that ancient and discoloured glass, the ruins of the chapel confronted me, bare and stark, in the yellow sunlight. I turned.

"There are no ghosts in the Abbey, I suppose, Mrs. Batty," I asked, whimsically.

But she took my inquiry very gravely. "I have never heard tell of one, Sir," she protested; "and if there was such a thing I should have known it."

As I was rejoining her a strange low whirring was audible, and looking up I saw in a corner of the high-arched roof a horrible face watching me out of black narrow eyes. I confess that I was very much startled at the apparition, but the next moment realised what it was. The creature hung with its ugly fleshy wings extended over a grotesque stone head that leered down upon me, its evil-looking snout projecting into the room; it lay perfectly still, returning me glance for glance, until moved by the repulsion of its presence I clapped my hands, and cried loudly; then, slowly flitting in a circle round the roof, it vanished with a flapping of wings into some darker corner of the rafters. Mrs. Batty was astounded, and expressed surprise that it had managed to conceal itself for so long.

"Oh, bats live in holes," I answered.

" Probably there is some small access through the masonry." But the incident had sent an uncomfortable shiver through me all the same.

Later that day I began to recognise that, short of an abrupt return to town, my time was not likely to be spent very pleasantly. But it was the personal problem so far as it concerned Warrington himself that distressed me even more. He came back from St. Pharamond in a morose and ugly temper, quite alien to his kindly nature. It seems that he had quarrelled bitterly with Miss Bosanquet, but upon what I could not determine, nor did I press him for an explanation. But the fumes of his anger were still rising when we met, and our dinner was a most depressing meal. He was in a degree of irritation which rendered it impossible to address him, and I soon withdrew into my thoughts. I saw, however, that he was drinking far too much, as, indeed, was plain subsequently when he invited me into the library. Once more he produced the hateful cards, and I was compelled to play, as he reminded me somewhat churlishly that I had promised him his revenge.

"Understand, Warrington," I said, firmly, "I play to-night, but never again, whatever the result. In fact, I am in half the mind to return to town to-morrow."

He gave me a look as he sct down, but said nothing, and the game began. He lost heavily from the first, and as nothing would content him but we must constantly raise the stakes, in a short time I had won several hundred pounds. He bore the reverses very ill, breaking out from time to time into some angry exclamation, now petulantly questioning my playing, and muttering oaths under his breath. But I was resolved that he should have no cause of complaint against me for this one night, and disregarding his insane fits of temper, I played steadily and silently. As the tally of my gains mounted he changed colour slowly, his face assuming a ghastly expression, and his eyes suspiciously denoting my actions. At length he rose, and throwing himself quickly across the table, seized my hand ferociously as I dealt a couple of cards.

" Damn you! I see your tricks," he cried, in frenzied passion. " Drop that hand, do you hear ? Drop that hand, or by——"

But he got no further, for, rising myself, I wrenched my hand from his grasp, and turned upon him, in almost as great a passion as himself. But suddenly, and even as I opened my mouth to speak, I stopped short with a cry of horror. His face was livid to the lips, his eyes were cast with blood, and upon the dirty white of his flesh, right in the centre of his throat, the round red scar, flaming and ugly as a wound, stared upon me.

" Warrington!" I cried, " what is this ?

What have you——" And I pointed in alarm to the spot.

" Mind your own business," he said, with a sneer. " It is well to try and draw off attention from your knavery. But that trick won't answer with me."

Without another word I flung the I O U's upon the table, and turning on my heel, left the room. I was furious with him, and fully resolved to leave the Abbey in the morning. I made my way upstairs to my room, and then, seating myself upon the balcony, endeavoured to recover my self-possession.

The more I considered, the more unaccountable was Warrington's behaviour. He had always been a perfectly courteous man, with a great lump of kindness in his nature, whereas these last few days he had been nothing other than a savage. It seemed certain that he must be ill or going mad; and as I reflected upon this the conjecture struck me with a sense of pity. If it was that he was losing his senses, how horrible was the tragedy in face of the new and lovely prospects opening in his life. Stimulated by this growing conviction, I resolved to go down and see him, more particularly as I now recalled his pleading voice that I should help him, on the previous evening. Was it not possible that this pathetic appeal derived from the instinct of the insane to protect themselves.

I found him still in the library; his head had fallen upon the table, and the state of the whisky bottle by his arm showed only too clearly his condition. I shook him vigorously, and he opened his eyes.

"Warrington, you must go to bed," I said.

He smiled, and greeted me quite affectionately. Obviously he was not so drunk as I had supposed.

"What is the time, Ned?" he asked.

I told him it was one o'clock, at which he rose briskly.

"Lord, I've been asleep," he said.
"Help me, Ned. I don't think I'm sober.
Where have you been?"

I assisted him to his room, and he un-
dressed slowly, and with an effort. Somehow, as I stood watching him, I yielded to
an unknown impulse, and said, suddenly:

"Warrington, don't sleep here. Come
and share my room."

"My dear fellow," he replied, with a
foolish laugh, "yours is not the only room
in the house. I can use half-a-dozen if I
like."

"Well, use one of them," I answered.

He shook his head. "I'm going to sleep
here," he returned, obstinately.

I made no further effort to influence him,
for, after all, now that the words were out,
I had absolutely no reason to give him or
myself for my proposition. And so I left
him. When I had closed the door, and was
turning to go along the passage, I heard

very clearly, as it seemed to me, a plaintive cry, muffled and faint, but very disturbing, which sounded from the room. Instantly I opened the door again. Warrington was in bed, and the heavy sound of his breathing told me that he was asleep. It was impossible that he could have uttered the cry. A night-light was burning by his bedside, shedding a strong illumination over the immediate vicinity, and throwing antic shadows on the walls. As I turned to go, there was a whirring of wings, a brief flap behind me, and the room was plunged in darkness. The obscene creature that lived in the recesses of the roof must have knocked out the tiny light with its wings. Then Warrington's breathing ceased, and there was no sound at all. And then once more the silence seemed to gather round me slowly and heavily, and whisper to me. I had a vague sense of being prevailed upon, of being enticed and lured by something in the surrounding air; a sort

of horror circumscribed me, and I broke
from the invisible ring and rushed from the
room. The door clanged behind me, and
as I hastened along the hall, once more
there seemed to ring in my ears the faint
and melancholy cry.

I awoke, in the sombre twilight that pre-
cedes the dawn, from a sleep troubled and
encumbered with evil dreams. The birds
had not yet begun their day, and a vast
silence brooded over the Abbey gardens.
Looking out of my window, I caught sight
of a dark figure stealing cautiously round
the corner of the ruined chapel. The furtive gait, as well as the appearance of a man
at that early hour, struck me with surprise;
and hastily throwing on some clothes, I ran
downstairs, and, opening the hall-door, went
out. When I reached the porch which gave
entrance to the aisle I stopped suddenly,
for there before me, with his head to the
ground, and peering among the tall grasses,

was the object of my pursuit. Then I stepped quickly forward and laid a hand upon his shoulder. It was Warrington.

" What are you doing here ?" I asked.

He turned and looked at me in bewilderment. His eyes wore a dazed expression, and he blinked in perplexity before he replied.

" It's you, is it ?" he said weakly. " I thought——" and then paused. " What is it ?" he asked.

" I followed you here," I explained. " I only saw your figure, and thought it might be some intruder."

He avoided my eyes. " I thought I heard a cry out here," he answered.

" Warrington," I said, with some earnestness, " come back to bed."

He made no answer, and slipping my arm in his, I led him away. On the door-step he stopped, and lifted his face to me.

" Do you think it's possible——" he

began, as if to inquire of me, and then again paused. With a slight shiver he proceeded to his room, while I followed him. He sat down upon his bed, and his eyes strayed to the barred window absently. The black shadow of the chapel was visible through the panes.

"Don't say anything about this," he said, suddenly. "Don't let Marion know."

I laughed, but it was an awkward laugh.

"Why, that you were alarmed by a cry for help, and went in search like a gentleman?" I asked, jestingly.

"You heard it, then?" he said, eagerly.

I shook my head, for I was not going to encourage his fancies. "You had better go to sleep," I replied, "and get rid of these nightmares."

He sighed and lay back upon his pillow, dressed as he was. Ere I left him he had fallen into a profound slumber.

If I had expected a surly mood in him

at breakfast I was much mistaken. There
was not a trace of his nocturnal dissipations;
he did not seem even to remember them,
and he made no allusion whatever to our
adventure in the dawn. He perused a letter
carefully, and threw it over to me with a
grin.

"Lor', what queer sheep women are!"
he exclaimed, with rather a coarse laugh.

I glanced at the letter without thinking,
but ere I had read half of it I put it aside.
It was certainly not meant for my eyes, and
I marvelled at Warrington's indelicacy in
making public, as it were, that very private
matter. The note was from Miss Bosanquet, and was clearly designed for his own
heart, couched as it was in the terms of
warm and fond affection. No man should
see such letters save he for whom they are
written.

"You see, they're coming over to dine,"
he remarked, carelessly. "Trust a girl to

make it up if you let her alone long enough.''

I made no answer; but though Warrington's grossness irritated me, I reflected with satisfaction upon his return to good humour, which I attributed to the reconciliation.

When I moved out upon the terrace the maid had entered to remove the breakfast things. I was conscious of a slight exclamation behind me, and Warrington joined me presently, with a loud guffaw.

'' That's a damned pretty girl!'' he said, with unction. '' I'm glad Mrs. Batty got her. I like to have good-looking servants.''

I suddenly interpreted the incident, and shrugged my shoulders.

'' You're a perfect boor this morning, Warrington,'' I exclaimed, irritably.

He only laughed. '' You're a dull dog of a saint, Heywood,'' he retorted. '' Come along,'' and dragged me out in no amiable spirit.

I had forgotten how perfect a host Warrington could be, but that evening he was
displayed at his best. The Bosanquets arrived early. Sir William was an easy-going
man, fond of books and of wine, and I now
guessed at the taste which had decided Warrington's cellar. Miss Bosanquet was as
charming as I remembered her to be; and if
any objection might be taken to Warrington
himself by my anxious eyes it was merely
that he seemed a trifle excited, a fault
which, in the circumstances, I was able to
condone. Sir William hung late about the
table, sipping his wine. Warrington, who
had been very abstemious, grew restless,
and, finally apologising in his graceful way,
left me to keep the baronet company. I
was the less disinclined to do so as I was
anxious not to intrude upon the lovers, and
Sir William was discussing the history of
the Abbey. He had an old volume somewhere in his library which related to it, and,

seeing that I was interested, invited me to look it up.

We sat long, and it was not until later that the horrible affair which I must narrate occurred.   The evening was close and oppressive, owing to the thunder, which already rumbled far away in the south. When we rose we found that Warrington and Miss Bosanquet were in the garden, and thither we followed.   As at first we did not find them, Sir William, who had noted the approaching storm with some uneasiness, left me to make arrangements for his return; and I strolled along the paths by myself, enjoying a cigarette.   I had reached the shrubbery upon the further side of the chapel, when I heard the sound of voices— a man's rough and rasping, a woman's pleading and informed with fear.   A sharp cry ensued, and without hesitation I plunged through the thicket in the direction of the speakers.   The sight that met me appalled me for the moment. Darkness was falling, lit with ominous flashes; and the two figures stood out distinctly in the bushes, in an attitude of struggle. I could not mistake the voices now. I heard Warrington's, brusque with anger, and almost savage in its tones, crying, " You shall!" and there followed a murmur from the girl, a little sob, and then a piercing cry. I sprang forward and seized Warrington by the arm; when, to my horror, I perceived that he had taken her wrist in both hands and was roughly twisting it, after the cruel habit of schoolboys. The malevolent cruelty of the action so astounded me that for an instant I remained motionless; I almost heard the bones in the frail wrist cracking; and then, in a second, I had seized Warrington's hands in a grip of iron, and flung him violently to the ground. The girl fell with him, and as I picked her up he rose too, and, clenching his fists, made as though to come at me, but

instead turned and went sullenly, and with
a ferocious look of hate upon his face, out
of the thicket.

Miss Bosanquet came to very shortly, and
though the agony of the pain must have
been considerable to a delicate girl, I believe
it was rather the incredible horror of the
act under which she swooned. For my part
I had nothing to say: not one word relative
to the incident dared pass my lips. I inquired if she was better, and then, putting
her arm in mine, led her gently towards the
house. Her heart beat hard against me, and
she breathed heavily, leaning on me for
support. At the chapel I stopped, feeling
suddenly that I dare not let her be seen in
this condition, and bewildered greatly by
the whole atrocious business.

" Come and rest in here," I suggested,
and we entered the chapel.

I set her on a slab of marble, and stood
waiting by her side. I talked fluently about

anything; for lack of a subject, upon the
tate of the chapel and the curious tomb
I had discovered. Recovering a little, she
joined presently in my remarks. It was
plain that she was putting a severe restraint
upon herself. I moved aside the grasses,
and read aloud the inscription on Sir
Rupert's grave-piece, and turning to the
next, which was rankly overgrown, feigned
to search further. As I was bending there,
suddenly, and by what thread of thought I
know not, I identified the spot with that
upon which I had found Warrington stooping that morning. With a sweep of my
hand I brushed back the weeds, uprooting
some with my fingers, and kneeling in the
twilight, pored over the monument. Suddenly a wild flare of light streamed down
the sky, and a great crash of thunder followed. Miss Bosanquet started to her feet
and I to mine. The heaven was lit up,
as it were, with sunlight, and, as I turned,

my eyes fell upon the now uncovered
stone.   Plainly the lettering flashed in my
eyes:

" *Priscilla, Lady Marvyn.*"

Then the clouds opened, and the rain fell
in spouts, shouting and dancing upon the
ancient roof overhead.

We were under a very precarious shelter,
and I was uneasy that Miss Bosanquet
should run the risk of that flimsy, ravaged
edifice; and so in a momentary lull I managed to get her to the house.   I found Sir
William in a restless state of nerves.   He
was a timorous man, and the thunder had
upset him, more particularly as he and his
daughter were now storm-bound for some
time.   There was no possibility of ventur-
ing into those rude elements for an hour or
more.   Warrington was not inside, and no
one had seen him.   In the light Miss Bosanquet's face frightened me; her eyes were
large and scared, and her colour very dead

white.   Clearly she was very near a break-down.   I found Mrs. Batty, and told her that the young lady had been severely shaken by the storm, suggesting that she had better lie down for a little.   Returning with me, the housekeeper led off the unfor-tunate girl, and Sir William and I were left together.   He paced the room impatiently, and constantly inquired if there were any signs of improvement in the weather.   He also asked for Warrington, irritably.   The burden of the whole dreadful night seemed fallen upon me.   Passing through the hall I met Mrs. Batty again.   Her usually placid features were disturbed and aghast.

" What is the matter ? " I asked.   " Is Miss Bosanquet——"

" No, Sir; I think she's sleeping," she replied.   " She's in—she is in Mr. Warring-ton's room."

I started.   " Are there no other rooms ? " I asked, abruptly.

"There are none ready, Sir, except yours," she answered, "and I thought——"

"You should have taken her there," I said, sharply. The woman looked at me and opened her mouth. "Good heavens!" I said, irritably, "what is the matter? Everyone is mad to-night."

"Alice is gone, Sir," she blurted forth.

Alice, I remembered, was the name of one of her maids.

"What do you mean?" I asked, for her air of panic betokened something graver than her words. The thunder broke over the house and drowned her voice.

"She can't be out in this storm—she must have taken refuge somewhere," I said.

At that the strings of ·her tongue loosened, and she burst forth with her tale. It was an abominable narrative.

"Where is Mr. Warrington?" I asked; but she shook her head.

There was a moment's silence between us,

and we eyed each other aghast. "She will be all right," I said at last, as if dismissing the subject.

The housekeeper wrung her hands. "I never would have thought it!" she repeated, dismally. "I never would have thought it!"

"There is some mistake," I said; but, somehow, I knew better. Indeed, I felt now that I had almost been prepared for it.

"She ran towards the village," whispered Mrs. Batty. "God knows where she was going! The river lies that way."

"Pooh!" I exclaimed. "Don't talk nonsense. It is all a mistake. Come, have you any brandy?"

Brought back to the material round of her duties she bustled away with a sort of briskness, and returned with a flagon and glasses. I took a strong nip, and went back to Sir William. He was feverish, and declaimed against the weather unceasingly. I had to listen to the string of misfortunes which he recounted in the season's crops. It seemed all so futile, with his daughter involved in her horrid tragedy in a neighbouring room. He was better after some brandy, and grew more cheerful, but assiduously wondered about Warrington.

"Oh, he's been caught in the storm and taken refuge somewhere," I explained, vainly. I wondered if the next day would ever dawn.

By degrees the thunder rolled slowly into the northern parts of the sky, and only fitful flashes seamed the heavens. It had lasted now more than two hours. Sir William declared his intention of starting, and asked for his daughter. I rang for Mrs. Batty, and sent her to rouse Miss Bosanquet. Almost immediately there was a knock upon the door, and the housekeeper was in the doorway, with an agitated expression, demanding to see me. Sir William was looking out of the window, and fortunately did not see her.

" Please come to Miss Bosanquet, Sir," she cried, very scared. " Please come at once."

In alarm I hastily ran down the corridor and entered Warrington's room. The girl was lying upon the bed, her hair flowing upon the pillow; her eyes, wide open and filled with terror, stared at the ceiling, and her hands clutched and twined in the coverlet as if in an agony of pain. A gasping sound issued from her, as though she were struggling for breath under suffocation. Her whole appearance was as of one in the murderous grasp of an assailant.

I bent over. " Throw the light, quick," I called to Mrs. Batty; and as I put my hand on her shoulder to lift her, the creature that lived in the chamber rose suddenly from the shadow upon the further side of the bed, and sailed with a flapping noise up to the cornice. With an exclamation of horror I pulled the girl's head forward, and the candle-light glowed on her pallid face. Upon the soft flesh of the slender throat was a round red mark, the size of a florin.

At the sight I almost let her fall upon the pillow again; but, commanding my nerves, I put my arms round her, and, lifting her bodily from the bed, carried her from the room. Mrs. Batty followed.

" What shall we do ? " she asked, in a low voice.

" Take her away from this damned chamber!" I cried. " Anywhere—the hall, the kitchen rather."

I laid my burden upon a sofa in the dining-room, and, despatching Mrs. Batty for the brandy, gave Miss Bosanquet a draught. Slowly the horror faded from her eyes; they closed, and then she looked at me.

" What have you ?—where am I ? " she asked.

" You have been unwell," I said. " Pray don't disturb yourself yet."

She shuddered, and closed her eyes again.

Very little more was said. Sir William pressed for his horses, and as the sky was clearing I made no attempt to detain him, more particularly as the sooner Miss Bosanquet left the Abbey the better for herself. In half an hour she recovered sufficiently to go, and I helped her into the carriage. She never referred to her seizure, but thanked me for my kindness. That was all. No one asked after Warrington—not even Sir William. He had forgotten everything, save his anxiety to get back. As the carriage turned from the steps I saw the mark upon the girl's throat, now grown fainter.

I waited up till late into the morning, but there was no sign of Warrington when I went to bed. Nor had he made his appearance when I descended to breakfast. A letter in his handwriting, however, and with the London postmark, awaited me. It was a pitiful scrawl, in the very penmanship of which one might trace the desperate emotions by which he was torn. He implored my forgiveness. "*Am I a devil?*" he asked. "*Am I mad? It was not I! It was not I!*" he repeated, underlining the sentence with impetuous dashes. "*You know*," he wrote; "*and you know, therefore, that everything is at an end for me. I am going abroad to-day. I shall never see the Abbey again.*"

It was well that he had gone, as I hardly think that I could have faced him; and yet I was loth myself to leave the matter in this horrible tangle. I felt that it was enjoined upon me to meet the problems, and I endeavoured to do so as best I might. Mrs. Batty gave me news of ·the girl Alice. It was bad enough, though not so bad as both of us had feared. I was able to make arrangements on the instant, which I hoped might bury that lamentable affair for the time. There remained Miss Bosanquet; but that difficulty seemed beyond me. I could see no avenue out of the tragedy. I heard nothing save that she was ill—an illness attributed upon all hands to the shock of exposure to the thunderstorm. Only I knew better, and a vague disinclination to fly from the responsibilities of the position kept me hanging on at Utterbourne.

It was in those days before my visit to St. Pharamond that I turned my attention more particularly to the thing which had forced itself relentlessly upon me. I was never a superstitious man; the gossip of old wives interested me merely as a curious and unsympathetic observer. And yet I was vaguely discomfited by the transaction in the Abbey, and it was with some reluctance that I decided to make a further test of Warrington's bedroom. Mrs. Batty received my determination to change my room easily enough, but with a protest as to the dampness of the Stone Chamber. It was plain that her suspicions had not marched with mine.   On the second night after Warrington's departure I occupied the room for the first time.

I lay awake for a couple of hours, with a reading lamp by my bed, and a volume of travels in my hand, and then, feeling very tired, put out the light and went to sleep. Nothing distracted me that night; indeed, I slept more soundly and peaceably than before in that house.   I rose, too, experiencing quite an exhilaration, and it was not until I was dressing before the glass that I remembered the circumstances of my mission; but then I was at once pulled up, startled swiftly out of my cheerful temper. Faintly visible upon my throat was the same round mark which I had already seen stamped upon Warrington and Miss Bosanquet.   With that, all my former doubts returned in force, augmented and militant. My mind recurred to the bat, and tales of bloodsucking by those evil creatures revived in my memory. But when I had remembered that these were of foreign beasts, and that I was in England, I dismissed them lightly enough. Still, the impress of that mark remained, and alarmed me. It could not come by accident; to suppose so manifold a coincidence was absurd. The puzzle dwelt with me, unsolved, and the fingers of dread slowly crept over me.

Yet I slept again in the room. Having but myself for company, and being somewhat bored and dull, I fear I took more spirit than was my custom, and the result was that I again slept profoundly. I awoke about three in the morning, and was surprised to find the lamp still burning. I had forgotten it in my stupid state of somnolence. As I turned to put it out, the bat swept by me and circled for an instant above my head. So overpowered with torpor was I that I scarcely noticed it, and my head was no sooner at rest than I was once more unconscious. The red mark was stronger next morning, though, as on the previous day, it wore off with the fall of evening. But I merely observed the fact without any concern; indeed, now the matter of my investigation seemed to have drawn very remote. I was growing indifferent, I supposed, through familiarity. But the solitude was palling upon me, and I spent a very restless day. A sharp ride I took in the afternoon was the one agreeable experience of the day. I reflected that if this burden were to continue I must hasten up to town. I had no desire to tie myself to Warrington's apron, in his interest. So dreary was the evening, that after I had strolled round the grounds and into the chapel by moonlight, I returned to the library and endeavoured to pass the time with Warrington's cards. But it was poor fun with no antagonist to pit myself against; and I was throwing down the pack in disgust when one of the men-servants entered with the whisky.

It was not until long afterwards that I fully realised the course of my action; but even at the time I was aware of a curious sub-feeling of shamefacedness. I am sure that the thing fell naturally, and that there was no awkwardness in my approaching him. Nor, after the first surprise, did he offer any objection. Later he was hardly expected to do so, seeing that he was winning very quickly. The reason of that I guessed afterwards, but during the play I was amazed to note at intervals how strangely my irritation was aroused. Finally, I swept the cards to the floor, and rose; the man, with a smile in which triumph blended with uneasiness, rose also.

"Damn you, get away!" I said, angrily.

True to his traditions to the close, he answered me with respect, and obeyed; and I sat staring at the table. With a sudden flush, the grotesque folly of the night's business came to me, and my eyes fell on the whisky bottle. It was nearly empty. Then I went to bed.

Voices cried all night in that chamber—soft, pleading voices. There was nothing to alarm in them; they seemed in a manner to coo me to sleep. But presently a sharper cry roused me from my semi-slumber; and getting up, I flung open the window. The wind rushed round the Abbey, sweeping with noises against the corners and gables. The black chapel lay still in the moonlight, and drew my eyes. But, resisting a strange, unaccountable impulse to go further, I went back to bed.

The events of the following day are better related without comment.

At breakfast I found a letter from Sir William Bosanquet, inviting me to come over to St. Pharamond. I was at once conscious of an eager desire to do so: it seemed somehow as though I had been waiting for this. The visit assumed preposterous proportions, and I was impatient for the afternoon.

Sir William was polite, but not, as I thought, cordial. He never alluded to Warrington, from which I guessed that he had been informed of the breach, and I conjectured also that the invitation extended to me was rather an act of courtesy to a solitary stranger than due to a desire for my company. Nevertheless, when he presently suggested that I should stay to dinner, I accepted promptly. For, to say the truth, I had not yet seen Miss Bosanquet, and I experienced a strange curiosity to do so. When at last she made her appearance, I was struck, almost for the first time, by her beauty. She was certainly a handsome girl, though she had a delicate air of ill-health.

After dinner Sir William remembered by

accident the book on the Abbey which he had promised to show me, and after a brief hunt in the library we found it. Shortly afterwards he was called away, and with an apology left me. With a curious eagerness I turned the pages of the volume and settled down to read.

It was published early in the century, and purported to relate the history of the Abbey and its owners. But it was one chapter which specially drew my interest—that which recounted the fate of the last Marvyn. The family had become extinct through a bloody tragedy; that fact held me. The bare narrative, long since passed from the memory of tradition, was here set forth in the baldest statements. The names of Sir Rupert Marvyn and Priscilla, Lady Marvyn, shook me strangely, but particularly the latter. Some links of connection with those gravestones lying in the Abbey chapel constrained me intimately. The history of that evil race was stained and discoloured with blood, and the end was in fitting harmony—a lurid holocaust of crime. There had been two brothers, but it was hard to choose between the foulness of their lives. If either, the younger, William, was the worse; so at least the narrative would have it. The details of his excesses had not survived, but it was abundantly plain that they were both notorious gamblers. The story of their deaths was wrapt in doubt, the theme of conjecture only, and probability; for none was by to observe save the three veritable actors— who were at once involved together in a bloody dissolution. Priscilla, the wife of Sir Rupert, was suspected of an intrigue with her brother-in-law. She would seem to have been tainted with the corruption of the family into which she had married. But according to a second rumour, chronicled by the author, there was some doubt if the woman were not the worst of the three.

Nothing was known of her parentage; she had returned with the passionate Sir Rupert to the Abbey after one of his prolonged absences, and was accepted as his legal wife. This was the woman whose infamous beauty had brought a terrible sin between the brothers.

Upon the night which witnessed the extinction of this miserable family, the two brothers had been gambling together. It was known from the high voices that they had quarrelled, and it is supposed that, heated with wine and with the lust of play, the younger had thrown some taunt at Sir Rupert in respect to his wife. Whereupon—but this is all conjecture—the elder stabbed him to death. At least, it was understood that at this point the sounds of a struggle were heard, and a bitter cry. The report of the servants ran that upon this noise Lady Marvyn rushed into the room and locked the door behind her. Fright was busy with those servants, long used to the savage manners of the house. According to witnesses, no further sound was heard subsequently to Lady Marvyn's entrance; yet when the doors were at last broken open by the authorities, the three bodies were discovered upon the floor.

How Sir Rupert and his wife met their death there was no record. "This tragedy," proceeded the scribe, "took place in the Stone Chamber underneath the stairway."

I had got so far when the entrance of Miss Bosanquet disturbed me. I remember rising in a dazed condition—the room swung about me. A conviction, hitherto resisted and stealthily entertained upon compulsion, now overpowered me.

"I thought my father was here," explained Miss Bosanquet, with a quick glance round the room.

I explained the circumstances, and she

hesitated in my neighbourhood with a slight air of embarrassment.

" I have not thanked you properly, Mr. Heywood," she said presently, in a low voice, scarcely articulate. " You have been very considerate and kind. Let me thank you now." And ended with a tiny spasmodic sob.

Somehow, an impulse overmastered my tongue. Fresh from the perusal of that chapter, queer possibilities crowded in my mind, odd considerations urged me.

" Miss Bosanquet," said I, abruptly, " let me speak of that a little. I will not touch on details."

" Please," she cried, with a shrinking notion as of one that would retreat in very alarm.

" Nay," said I, eagerly; " hear me. It is no wantonness that would press the memory upon you. You have been a witness to distressful acts; you have seen a man under the influence of temporary madness. Nay, even yourself, you have been a victim to the same unaccountable phenomena."

"What do you mean?" she cried, tensely.

"I will say no more," said I. "I should incur your laughter. No, you would not laugh, but my dim suspicions would leave you still incredulous. But if this were so, and if these were the phenomena of a brief madness, surely you would make your memory a grave to bury the past."

"I cannot do that," said she, in low tones.

"What!" I asked. "Would you turn from your lover, aye, even from a friend, because he was smitten with disease? Consider; if your dearest upon earth tossed in a fever upon his bed, and denied you in his ravings, using you despitefully, it would not be he that entreated you so. When he was quit of his madness and returned to his proper person, would you not forget—would you not rather recall his insanity with the pity of affection ?"

" I do not understand you," she whispered.

" You read your Bible," said I. " You have wondered at the evil spirits that possessed poor victims. Why should you decide that these things have ceased ? We are too dogmatic in our modern world. Who can say under what malign influence a soul may pass, and out of its own custody ?"

She looked at me earnestly, searching my eyes.

" You hint at strange things," said she, very low.

But somehow, even as I met her eyes, the spirit of my mission failed me. My gaze, I felt, devoured her ruthlessly. The light shone on her pale and comely features; they burned me with an irresistible attraction. I put forth my hand and took hers gently.

It was passive to my touch, as though in acknowledgment of my kindly offices. All the while I experienced a sense of fierce elation. In my blood ran, as it had been fire, a horrible incentive, and I knew that I was holding her hand very tightly. She herself seemed to grow conscious of this, for she made an effort to withdraw her fingers, at which, the passion rushing through my body, I clutched them closer, laughing aloud. I saw a wondering look dawn in her eyes, and her bosom, thinly veiled, heaved with a tiny tremor. I was aware that I was drawing her steadily to me. Suddenly her bewildered eyes, dropping from my face, lit with a flare of terror, and, wrenching her hand away, she fell back with a cry, her gaze riveted upon my throat.

" That accursed mark! What is it ? What is it?——" she cried, shivering from head to foot.

In an instant, the wild blood singing in

my head, I sprang towards her. What would·have followed I know not, but at that moment the door opened and Sir William returned. He regarded us with consternation; but Miss Bosanquet had fainted, and the next moment he was at her side. I stood near, watching her come to with a certain nameless fury, as of a beast cheated of its prey. Sir William turned to me, and in his most courteous manner begged me to excuse the untoward scene. His daughter, he said, was not at all strong, and he ended by suggesting that I should leave them for a time.

Reluctantly I obeyed, but when I was out of the house, I took a sudden panic. The demoniac possession lifted, and in a craven state of trembling I saddled my horse, and rode for the Abbey as if my life depended upon my speed.

I arrived at about ten o'clock, and immediately gave orders to have my bed pre-

pared in my old room. In my shaken condition the sinister influences of that stone
chamber terrified me; and it was not until
I had drunk deeply that I regained my
composure.

But I was destined to get little sleep. I
had steadily resolved to keep my thoughts
off the matter until the morning, but the
spell of the chamber was strong upon me.
I awoke after midnight with an irresistible
feeling drawing me to the room. I was conscious of the impulse, and combated it, but
in the end succumbed; and throwing on my
clothes, took a light and went downstairs.
I flung wide the door of the room and
peered in, listening, as though for some
voice of welcome. It was as silent as a
sepulchre; but directly I crossed the threshold voices seemed to surround and coax me.
I stood wavering, with a curious fascination
upon me. I knew I could not return to my
own room, and I now had no desire to do

so.   As I stood, my candle flaring solemnly against the darkness, I noticed upon the floor in an alcove bare of carpet, a large black mark, which appeared to be a stain.   Bending down, I examined it, passing my fingers over the stone.   It moved to my touch. Setting the candle upon the floor, I put my finger-tips to the edges, and pulled hard. As I did so the sounds that were ringing in my ears died instantaneously; the next moment the slab turned with a crash, and discovered a gaping hole of impenetrable blackness.

The patch of chasm thus opened to my eyes was near a yard square.   The candle held to it shed a dim light upon a stone step a foot or two below, and it was clear to me that a stairway communicated with the depths.   Whether it had been used as a cellar in times gone by I could not divine, but I was soon to determine this doubt; for, stirred by a strange eagerness, I slipped my legs through the hole, and let myself cautiously down with the light in my hand. There were a dozen steps to descend ere I reached the floor and what turned out to be a narrow passage. The vault ran forward straight as an arrow before my eyes, and slowly I moved on. Dank and chill was the air in those close confines, and the sound of my feet returned from those walls dull and sullen. But I kept on, and, with infinite care, must have penetrated quite a hundred yards along that musty corridor ere I came out upon an ampler chamber. Here the air was freer, and I could perceive with the aid of my light that the dimensions of the place were lofty. Above, a solitary ray of moonlight, sliding through a crack, informed me that I was not far from the level of the earth. It fell upon a block of stone, which rose in the middle of the vault, and which I now inspected with interest. As the candle threw its flickering beams upon this I

realised where I was. I scarcely needed
the rude lettering upon the coffins to ac-
quaint me that here was the family vault of
the Marvyns. And now I began to perceive
upon all sides whereon my feeble light fell
the crumbling relics of the forgotten dead—
coffins fallen into decay, bones and grinning
skulls resting in corners, disposed by the
hand of chance and time. This formidable
array of the mortal remains of that poor
family moved me to a shudder. I turned
from those ugly memorials once more to
the central altar where the two coffins rested
in this sombre silence. The lid had fallen
from the one, disclosing to my sight the
grisly skeleton of a man, that mocked and
leered at me. It seemed in a manner to my
fascinated eyes to challenge my mortality,
inviting me too to the rude and grotesque
sleep of death. I knew, as by an instinct,
that I was standing by the bones of Sir Rupert Marvyn, the protagonist in that terrible

crime which had locked three souls in eternal ruin. The consideration of this miserable spectacle held me motionless for some moments, and then I moved a step closer and cast my light upon the second coffin.

As I did so I was aware of a change within myself. The grave and melancholy thoughts which I had entertained, the sober bent of my solemn reflections, gave place instantly to a strange exultation, an unholy sense of elation. My pulse swung feverishly, and, while my eyes were riveted upon the tarnished silver of the plate, I stretched forth a tremulously eager hand and touched the lid. It rattled gently under my fingers. Disturbed by the noise, I hastily withdrew them; but whether it was the impetus offered by my touch, or through some horrible and nameless circumstance—God knows—slowly and softly a gap opened between the lid and the body of the coffin! Before my startled eyes the awful thing happened, and yet I was conscious of no terror, merely of surprise and—it seems terrible to admit —of a feeling of eager expectancy. The lid rose slowly on the one side, and as it lifted the dark space between it and the coffin grew gently charged with light. At that moment my feeble candle, which had been gradually diminishing, guttered and flickered. I seemed to catch a glimpse of something, as it were, of white and shining raiment inside the coffin; and then came a rush of wings and a whirring sound within the vault. I gave a cry, and stepping back missed my foothold; the guttering candle was jerked from my grasp, and I fell prone to the floor in darkness. The next moment a sheet of flame flashed in the chamber and lit up the grotesque skeletons about me; and at the same time a piercing cry rang forth. Jumping to my feet, I gave a dazed glance at the conflagration. The whole vault was in flames. Dazed and horror-struck, I rushed blindly to the entrance; but as I did so the horrible cry pierced my ears again, and I saw the bat swoop round and circle swiftly into the flames. Then, finding the exit, I dashed with all the speed of terror down the passage, groping my way along the walls, and striking myself a dozen times in my terrified flight.

Arrived in my room, I pushed over the stone and listened. Not a sound was audible. With a white face and a body torn and bleeding I rushed from the room, and locking the door behind me, made my way upstairs to my bedroom. Here I poured myself out a stiff glass of brandy.

*　　*　　*　　*　　*

It was six months later ere Warrington returned. In the meantime he had sold the Abbey. It was inevitable that he should do so; and yet the new owner, I believe, has found no drawback in his property, and the Stone Chamber is still used for a bedroom upon occasions, being considered very old-fashioned.   But there are some facts against which no appeal is possible, and so it was in his case.   In my relation of the tragedy I have made no attempt at explanation, hardly even to myself; and it appears now for the first time in print, of course with suppositious names.

IV

Zoraka

THE disposition of the evening was pleasant, but somehow a feeling of restless discontent prevailed upon me. It was as if I had tired of the extravagant picturesqueness of the East. The barbaric interest of the bazaars, the unfamiliar brightness of the streets, the pied and variegated throngs—all these seemed now to pass, as with the distance and seclusion of a stereoscopic vision. I looked down, as it were, upon coloured plates, picked out with shifting scenes, in which I was a stranger with no part. This turbaned mob passed to and fro about its affairs; it held markets, chaffered in the public emporiums, offered solemn greetings;

and I myself was admitted to these commercial and polite exchanges. But that was all. The real life of the people lay wide apart from their business appearances day by day. From that I was excluded. Saving for the change of colour and feature it might as well be a cockney quarter of London I was regarding, or the smart round of life upon the Boulevards. This sequestration had come at last to annoy me, and the aspects of the town wore now almost the familiarity of my native suburb. The disappointment settled in monotony; even the novelty of the living had grown stale, and the wine which at first had drunk very strangely and quite agreeably to the palate, was now revealed as merely thin and sour, as like a tenpenny Bordeaux as may be, and not so wholesome.

These reflections occupied me in my chamber in the caravanserai, as I looked forth of the window upon the huge white walls and the green gardens they held so private. The sun had gone down, but his influences were still flaming in the West; a little night-air, soft and soothing, was beginning to stir, and the tamarisks were waving quietly. The spring was still young. Behind such walls as those the lives of these Orientals were exhibited in the fulness of their blood. There such romances as they knew dawned and died; the comedies and tragedies of their passions were enacted there no less than in Bayswater drawing-rooms or Kensington boudoirs. It fretted me to feel that from a journey such as mine had been one might take no more than the knowledge to be thrown from a lantern-slide—the public processions, the investing rags, the sardonic faces of an unknown and passionate race.

1 looked across the street below my window to the wall which closed my immediate purview. The figure of a tall man, in the full particulars of native costume, moved

slowly, and as it struck me, with an air of stealth, along the little alley. The muezzin had just chanted the call to prayer sonorously from the minaret of a neighbouring mosque. Somehow, quite vaguely, I seemed to recall a previous recognition of this furtive figure; and then, in a moment, I knew what had tickled my memory. It was my custom at this hour, after the long hot day, to sit here at this loophole and look forth upon the street, and now I remembered that this same tall fellow was used to haunt the alley simultaneously upon the fall of the muezzin's voice. I sat up sharply and watched him with a hasty accession of interest. Why, here, maybe, was the very occasion of romance stalking past my doorway, and I unheeding. The fellow stopped before a door in the wall, and, with a surreptitious glance about him, pushed it open and disappeared within. I was feverish with unrest and dissatisfaction, and for some reason the secrecy of the act stirred a pleasant thrill in me. I half rose from my seat, moved by a sndden whim, and paused again. "Why, yes," said I to myself, laughing. "Why not?" My heart pulsed quickly. I was certainly in a way to be roused from my indifference. I put a revolver in my pocket, and, leaving the inn, walked quickly down the street, and, turning into the alley, stood in a few moments hesitating before the door just as my suspicious stranger himself had done.

To my surprise the door was slightly ajar. I was much under the influence of my imagination, but for a second or so I remained with my hand upon the woodwork, while my heart beat faster. Upon what high adventure was I at last bound? Or was it to end as a commonplace blunder, in smiles, bows, apologies, and perhaps a cup of coffee and a cigarette? The door moved noiselessly back, and I entered; the next moment it fell to behind me heavily, and I was in a dark passage. As my eyes adjusted themselves to the change I discerned a little way ahead a soft dull glow, as from a light piercing through thick curtains. Feeling upon the wall, I advanced towards this, and found myself at last upon the threshold of a room shut off from the passage, as I had supposed, by rich hangings. The chamber itself was empty, but by many marks I took it for the private apartment of a woman. Entering with some exaltation of spirit I was proceeding to make further explorations, when all of a sudden a footstep sounded at my back, and, turning, I beheld a large man of middle age standing in the curtained doorway. We regarded each other in silence, for indeed I was a good deal taken aback, but presently he spoke.

"You are welcome," he said, "I have been waiting for you."

His voice was without emotion of any

kind, nor had I any clue to what I was welcomed. Save for a certain excited light in his eyes he might have been the polite host his words would bespeak him.

"I am glad, sir," said I, making him a bow, "to have blundered thus upon your hospitality."

He made no response to my salutation, but clapped his hands abruptly. So immediately as to suggest that they had been in hiding near by, a couple of stalwart fellows jumped into the room, and ere I could divine their intention had their hands upon me. My revolver lay useless in my pocket, but I struggled for a moment ineffectually in their clutches, and then ceasing, indignantly demanded of the master what this meant.

"Is this the way," I asked, "to treat a guest, who has trespassed by inadvertence in your house?"

He made no reply, but in a voice, now

harsh and sounding with triumph, bade his men bring me after him. I was conducted through corridors out upon a court, which had plainly once possessed some magnificence, but had now fallen into disorder, the fountain alone remaining of its ancient splendour; and thence through a maze of passages into a large room, decorated with florid designs and barely furnished, as is the custom in these parts. Here, the master of the house seated himself upon a divan, and surveyed me for some moments with a curious look of savage satisfaction in his eyes, while I, in the hands of my guards, reviewed my position with amazement and alarm. In a little time the man clapped his hands again, and there entered presently a tall black, richly dressed, in whom I could not but recognise the chief eunuch of that household. He stared at me as if in great surprise, and then hurriedly approaching his master, whispered a few words. His looks betokened bewilderment, and indeed the effect of his communication served to derange my captor also.

" What is this ?" he said harshly. " Dog, do you lie to me ?" and glowered upon the black.

The eunuch salaamed humbly. " It is true, lord of our lives," he answered, " we have already captured the other."

His master frowned, but recovering, looked sardonically at me. " Bring them both," he commanded, " and the woman shall decide between them."

With that the eunuch disappeared, and when he returned he was accompanied by a commotion. I set eyes first upon the very man whom I had thus foolishly pursued into what I now began to perceive must be some trap, and he, like myself, was in the custody of servants. But after him followed the black, dragging rather than supporting the body of a very handsome woman with

black eyes and flowing hair. She was no
sooner entered than she threw herself before
the divan and embarked upon a passion of
tears and entreaties. So far as I could understand her language, for her voice was
broken with sobs, she protested against
some suspicion the man had taken of her,
and pleaded at once for his justice and his
mercy. And then it was that I began to
gather some dim hints of my own predicament. Zoraka, for so she called herself in
her piteous appeals, was the wife of this
Hassan, as she named him. The fellow
who was in custody with myself had plainly
been her lover, and, as I now conceived, I
had been so unfortunate as to make my silly
venture upon the very day on which Hassan
in his suspicion had chosen to lay a snare
for his wife's paramour. Into that net two
had fallen. The notion was so ludicrous,
when I considered it, that I could have
laughed out had it not been for the tragic

consequences that seemed pending. It would manifestly be no jest to stand before this creature's jealous fury. The woman had cast no glance upon us when she entered, and lay now in a grovelling attitude of supplication before her lord. To her prayers he paid not the slightest heed, and, at last, with a scowl pushed her from him with his foot. At which, appearing to understand that all was lost, she withdrew herself quickly and got upon her feet quite calmly. The sudden change in her demeanour startled me, used as I was to the shifting passions of the race. She stood impassive for a while as though resigned to her fate, and then, her gaze falling upon me, stared at me in sullen wonder. Glutted of his victim's miserable anticipations, Hassan now stirred on his couch. With Oriental phlegm he lighted a long pipe, and addressing my fellow-prisoner demanded in harsh tones what he was doing there. The man made some reply, in which moroseness mingled with terror, and then it was my turn.

"Sir," said I, "I know nothing of this woman or of this man. I am an innocent Feringhi who wandered through your doorway by mistake. I demand my release, or my Government will exact a heavy price at your hands."

A grim smile lit up his sour features, and he turned to the woman, Zoraka. "Accursed one," he said, "which of these is your lover, or are your passions so insatiable that you have taken both to your traitorous bosom?"

Zoraka shook her head. "They are strangers, my lord," she returned. "Why must I stand before strangers with my naked face?"

All the time her eyes watched me curiously. Hassan darted a terrible look of hate upon her.

"We will make sure of all three," he said, and made a sign to his eunuch.

The negro drew from a scabbard in the folds of his robe a huge scimitar, handling which in a familiar way he approached the woman. Her eyes still dwelt attentively upon me, and it was not until the black touched her roughly upon the shoulder that she seemed to be aware of his presence by her side. She started ever so slightly, and, glancing at the shining sword, shivered perceptibly. Then again, as though drawn by an irresistible magnet, her gaze returned to me. The menace of these proceedings struck me as so monstrous that for all I had heard of the cruel rigours of the harem law, I could not fully realise that any tragedy was proposed. I met her eyes, and in mine, I know, was a deep look of compassion for this beautiful creature. At this exchange of our glances she smiled softly, and turning slightly about, regarded the black with curling lips and flattened nostrils. Suddenly Hassan leapt from his seat and broke into the most frantic exhibition of brutal anger I have ever seen in a man. All his show of indifference was gone. He cast up his hands, with clenched fists, and raved like a maniac, denouncing Zoraka in the vilest terms, calling curses upon her future life, and blackening the character of her ancestors. The woman never flinched, and when his vituperation ceased from lack of breath, she addressed him.

" My lord," she said, with a certain dignity in her low and measured voice, " you hold the keys of Life and Death in this household. It is your will that I bare my neck here to Death upon this spot. Allah decrees it, and the Prophet assents. Think not that it is with any regret that I leave this world. My heart has been too full. I have been your plaything, the vehicle of your passion.

" We women," she cried with rising spirit, "are the prisoners of the harem.

It is our fortune. We are sold from out our birthright; we pass under foreign hands; we are the non-entities of pleasure. And lo, there is among us not even the little liberty of desire. If hope sparkle in my eyes and the light shine on my soul, whence have I offended against you? You cannot hush the throbbing of my heart; it rises under my bosom in the darkness of my chamber. As for these men, I know nothing of them. The sword is in your hands. Let them go."

She faced him with heaving breast but with a quiet face which won my admiration. But the effect of her rebuke upon Hassan was indescribable. His black face blanched with rage. He ran down the steps between them and seizing the scimitar from the eunuch made as though to strike off her head at a blow. I moved involuntarily, but my gaolers held me tight, and it seemed that the bloody scene must be enacted before my eyes, while I was powerless to move a hand. But as suddenly Hassan paused and withheld the knife from the stroke.

"No," said he, with a malign contortion of his features, "she shall be sprinkled first with the blood of her lovers. Bring the dogs forward."

We were hustled forward by our guards and brought within a pace or two of the ruffian, and Zoraka; once more she shot a glance at me, and once more I met it with a thrill of pity. The black took the scimitar from his master and drew near my companion. Almost for the first time I examined him closely. He was a fine-looking fellow, of some position, I judged, and bore himself very well in that supreme moment. His complexion was overcast with a sallow shade of fear, but he made neither sound nor sign, submitting himself to the butchers like a frightened sheep. The transaction had a dreadful fascination for me; it drew my eyes. I was entirely incapable of considering my own situation. The black came behind him and with a rude movement of his brawny arm twisted the man's head forward, so as to leave the neck bare and free. Then he gripped his scimitar and swung it in the air. I could not refrain a glance at Zoraka; but she stood motionless, watching with wide eyes, only a little tense contraction of the nostrils speaking to her emotion. The executioner raised his sword and a flash spread into a broad shaft of light. A sort of groan started from my lips, but Zoraka was dumb. Whether he had had instructions beforehand and knew his part in the devilish piece of cruelty I cannot say, but suddenly, and when to my eyes all was over and the awful bearded head already rolling upon the floor, the black's arms stopped dead, and the sword was arrested on the very skin of the man's neck. The eunuch looked at his master, and in obedience to a nod left the wretched, trembling creature and approached me.

I cannot tell how it was, but my mind grew lively all at once with a terrible illumination. In a flash I saw the meaning of this brutal scene; it was designed to betray the real lover by wresting a display of emotion from Zoraka. And with that a still more fearful thought rushed in upon me. I felt that I knew now with what purpose she had interrogated me so fully with her eyes. Her looks had been directed solely upon me; never for a second had she noticed her lover. It was upon me she desired to throw suspicion, in the hope to save the man she loved, even though she herself were sacrificed to her husband's wrath. I know not to what extent this manœuvre had been observed, but in the new horror of my discovery I feared the worst. And I was now to suffer the same trial as my fellow. For one instant the blood, rushing to my brain, blinded me. I saw Zoraka through a mist, and bestowed upon her a look of reproach and repugnance. Then I engaged in a fierce, futile struggle with my captors. Their arms pinioned me, and I was flung forward, helpless in their grasp. If I remember aright, I had just one wild animal desire to throw myself on Hassan and tear him in shreds, and then a numb apathy succeeded, and I was conscious only of waiting for Zoraka's cry. I heard dimly the scimitar hissing in the air, and simultaneously it seemed felt the wind and an edge across my neck; and then the scream of agony which I had anticipated. Next instant my guards pulled me back, and I was face to face with Zoraka, looking into my eyes with a genuine expression of terror. Was it possible, I vaguely wondered, that this cry had been wrung from her out of a real pity for an innocent victim? But then recalling her indifference, when her lover was at stake,

I dismissed the thought as absurd, and fell back upon my previous conviction of her cunning.

It was merely death that I expected now, and it was a short sharp death I prayed for. Yet it was horrible that I should have to undergo again the tortures of that lingering passage. But Hassan was silent and issued no order. He came down from the daïs and passed me by, searching my face with a swift puzzled look; then he proceeded to scrutinise my companion also. It was plain he was in doubt. Could it be that he, too, had a suspicion of Zoraka's trick? I came to the conclusion that this was so, for turning to the black he gave orders that we should be kept in custody till the morrow, adding with a filthy remark about his wife, that if the real lover were not disclosed by then, she should take both upon her bosom into Paradise. I daresay he had designed some horrid form of death for the paramour, which

made his identification a matter of anxiety;
for on that ground alone can I explain his
reluctance to despatch us all three by the
sword.

I was removed into a small chamber,
quite devoid of furniture, and with high-
barred windows as like a cell as might be,
save that the pure air of the gardens entered in wafts. And here I fell into a grave
consideration of my peril and remorse for
my foolhardiness. Since I had wanted the
romance of the East, why here was more
than my share of it at last, and very grubby
and abominable it was. I could be content,
I thought, after this, if there were any after
this, with the magic-lantern and stereoscopic
views of Oriental life. A Kodak was better
than a dungeon, and however picturesque
they sounded, mediæval conditions were not
suited to a Victorian man. They had de-
prived me of my revolver, but had left me
free, trusting, no doubt, to the solid ma-

sonry of the house.   Yet I wandered to and fro for hours, debating the possibilities of my escape, and framing a hundred plans for scaling the wall and breaking through the window.   By-and-bye, however, resignation settled upon me, as the hopelessness of these schemes was slowly revealed, and by this time, feeling quite worn out with my anxieties and the lateness of the hour, I fell asleep upon the bare boards of the floor.

Some time afterwards I was awakened by a touch on my shoulder, and sat up quickly. A soft melodious voice breathed in my ear.

" Hush ! " it said, " O Feringhi, be silent, lest the guards upon the courtyard hear you."

" Who are you ? " I cried, sleep struggling with my interest.

" It is I, Zoraka," said the voice, and indeed I recognized it now.   " It is I, O Light of my Eyes."

I do not know that the expression fell

upon very intelligent ears, for the fact was that I was bewildered with her presence there. "How came you here?" I asked in astonishment to find this victim, but lately designed and destined to death with me, thus moving free with all her liberties.

Zoraka laughed softly. "There is none that can keep me from my beloved," she whispered in her honeyed voice. "They encircled me, but I deceived them. They sleep soundly. Did the fool think to bind me and to still my heart? Listen how it beats for thee."

She was warming my hand gently, and now I became aware of her action, and there dawned upon me the significance of this strange visit. I was suddenly overwhelmed with the revelation. With the remarkable abruptness of Eastern passions, Zoraka had transferred her affections to me, moved by some unaccountable whim. The thought had never for an instant occurred to me, and now I sat silent, with my hand in hers, suffering her warm touch, and revolving in confusion this new development in my fortunes. There was a sound from the next room, and Zoraka clutched me tight. "Hush!" she murmured, with her finger to her lips, "we must leave, my beloved. Let us depart into the deep night and be gone. Stay!"

She moved quickly to the door, and as she passed from me the moonlight streamed through the window upon her lithe and graceful figure, stirring in me a curious sensation. She stood listening for a moment, and then beckoned me with her hand. I rose and followed her. The latch clicked softly, and we were in a gloomy passage. She moved forward, and I pursued her noiseless footsteps, traversing many silent rooms and ill-lit corridors, until at length we came out into a place where the light was clearer and I could smell the fresh air of a garden. Here she stopped and pointed to an open door.

"Go forth," she whispered, "and wait for me. I will return. We must go armed"; and with a swish of her robes was gone.

I walked out into the garden, still under the spell of my amazement; the night was thick with stars and a yellow moon; the soft fragrance of earth was in my nostrils. Here was the way to safety; the open garden lay before reaching to the lane; I was free.

Suddenly I heard, piercing from some inner chamber and muffled by distance, a sharp wailing cry.

The sound arrested me. It rose, a thin high wail, and died without echoes in the night. For a time I stood listening for a repetition of the cry, but none came, and silence presided alike in the house and in the garden, save for the breaths of air that stirred among the leaves. That discomfortable shriek awoke conjecture in me instantly, and under the shadow of the arbutus impulses and emotions divided me. Away, at the foot of the garden, the stars danced lightly in the waters of the bay, inviting me to flight. The term of that intestine conflict in my thoughts was considerable, but in the end I came out of my shelter and retraced my way back into the house. I had an indefinite sense of pleasure in my magnanimity, mingling simultaneously with a feeling that I was under an obligation of honour not to desert Zoraka.

The house was still and dark as upon my journey forth. When I came to consider, my adventure was in no wise heroic, but merely fatuous. I had no manner of notion where Zoraka lay, nor indeed if she had not been already sacrificed to the ferocious passions of her husband. That might have been the real significance of her anguished scream. And even if I had all uncertainties determined, my quest was no more reasonable. To snatch her from the centre of her guards and bring into safety—the idea was preposterous.   Yet in a little I should have been quite at a loss to retreat, if I had desired to do so, for I was soon involved in a labyrinth of darkened chambers. Passage opened into passage, and corridor succeeded corridor.   I walked with great secrecy, and listened with both ears alert.   At one time I caught near-by the plash of a fountain, and guessed that I must be somewhere within the vicinity of the interior court.   If that were so, I had wandered a long way from the garden.   It was strange that I encountered no one; the house seemed wrapt in the quiet of the tombs.   Once in my passage through a room I heard the slow and even noise of sleepers, but no person barred my way.   My progress was necessarily difficult, for I had little light to guide me, and must for the most part grope my way through blackness.   I began to despair at last of finding any exit from this gloomy prison.   Zoraka insensibly faded from my imagination; the hunt for her seemed supremely foolish with no clue to direct me. And I had now the oppression of my own fresh peril upon me. It was upon these reflections that I came at length into a large chamber, which sounded bare and vacant to my tread. Fingering on the wall I moved carefully round it, in search of the further doorway, for the apartments in these houses invariably communicated with one another. My chagrin reached its height when I was unable to discover any door; nor was this the worst, for upon retiring the way I had come, I found that the door by which I had entered had completely vanished. The darkness, I suppose, confused me; the chamber was probably of an unusual shape; at any rate I seemed to make the circuit a dozen times without success. I was incarcerated within those solid walls as securely as if the bars of a prison held me. As I made this desperate comment to myself, I stumbled over a couch, and putting forth my hands to save a fall was flung heavily upon some human body that lay thereon.

I withdrew hastily, and in a whirl of fears; but no start or exclamation followed, and I recalled now, as I stood, thick with apprehensions, that the face had been cold and dry to the touch. This with the curious stillness reassured me that my terror was groundless; it was a corpse that reposed in the calm silence of that darkness. The thought informed me with a new feeling of distaste. A strange impulse led me to stretch out my hand again, and touch the body in a gingerly fashion. I was conscious that my fingers were wetted and cold, and I drew off sharply with a shudder. In my mind speculations, which were almost convictions, broke vaguely and unpleasantly. I was interrupted in my horrid considerations by the sound of feet, the first sound of positive life that had yet reached me. I fled in haste, and by sheer good fortune ran into a heavy curtain that draped the wall hard by. I had scarcely wrapped myself in the folds of this when a light burst into the room, and two ill-looking fellows entered and proceeded to the couch. The light illumined the dead man's face, and showed me that my conjecture had been right—Zoraka's lover lay there, stretched out in the ugly peace of death. Save for a sinister contraction of the nostrils, and the protrusion of a yellow tooth above the underlip, the countenance was underanged by his violent end; and only a streak of blood stained the beard. I will confess that I dared not look upon this scene without emotion; the accomplishment of the tragedy persisted in my thoughts and challenged me with its menace. I had few doubts at this moment that Zoraka too had perished, and I, fool that I was, had hazarded my chance of safety almost beyond retrieval.

The servants raised the body without any signs of interest, and carrying it between them toiled across the room towards the door, which I now perceived was hidden behind the arras. When they had disappeared I followed furtively. Almost the first step I took, I tripped upon some hard substance on the floor, and stooping discovered to my satisfaction that it was a knife. Here at any rate was a useful ally in my predicament. Concealing it about me I pursued after the men, for in them, it appeared, lay my only prospect of finding a way out of the house. But here fell my second surprise. I maintained my course at a considerable distance from the fellows, who had little chance of detecting me from the noise they made under their burden, and presently saw them push open a door in the corridor and disappear. I hastened my steps, and just as I reached the door a wild shriek rang out of the silence.

Zoraka

This, then was news of Zoraka; but what news ? Eagerly, and with trepidant heart, I thrust open the door behind its hangings, and peered into the room. It was well lighted. The two men had come to a halt and laid their burden upon the floor. But it was not upon these my gaze lingered, but upon the tall figure of the Nubian eunuch, who was contemplating with an indifferent and cruel smile the prostrate body of Zoraka. She lay upon her back upon the mosaic, with her arms flung out, and for a moment (so devilish did the scene present itself to my imagination) I was on the point of throwing myself upon the black, knife in hand. But this impulse passed, and the next second, at a loud signal from him, a fourth man entered, bearing a large sheet of sacking. With a gathering sense of dread I stared from him to Zoraka's body, and as my eyes lit upon her, I noticed her bosom slowly rising, as if with a resumption of.

life.   It was a relief to find that she was not
dead, as I had imagined, though I could not
but conjecture that some outrage was intended.   I was soon to be enlightened as
to the black's purpose, for at his instructions the three ruffians proceeded to bind
the two bodies together, the living body of
Zoraka with the stiff and clammy corpse of
her hapless lover.   The act seemed a hide-
ous profanation, but I was helpless before
this abominable company, even though I
feared that worse was yet to fall.   Before
my eyes the living and the dead were enwrapped together in the sacking and secured
with thick cords.   If they had been undivided in their lives, I could imagine Hassan
sneering, so surely should they remain un-
separated in death; and she at least was
free to awake upon her lover's bosom in
Paradise.

 Zoraka had stirred slightly but had not
recovered consciousness ere she was lashed

in this contumelious bundle. When the work was complete the party, headed by the black, moved out of the apartment, the three men with the sacking supported between them. Concealing myself in a dark corner of the passage I watched the procession; it passed me laboriously, and, after a safe interval, I slipped out and followed. This time I was certain of gaining the open air, for I knew well enough the destination of those poor victims. The ancient order of this venerable kingdom suffers no change, and the bay now, as ever, buries its secrets fathoms deep. In this fashion we came presently upon the garden, and once more the delicious breath of heaven animated my lungs. But now that my private fears were allayed, again my sympathy turned to the unfortunate woman designed for this atrocious end. I followed still, until the company reached the base of the garden and the bay. A low wall here set a bound to the dark water, and mounting upon this the four came to a halt, with their monstrous package resting upon the stone. I watched with an unnatural eagerness from the cover of the thick bushes below. At a signal from the eunuch the others raised the sacking, and swaying and swinging for a moment upon the ledge, then swiftly flung their arms seaward. With a great thud and a splash the bodies struck the water, while the spray danced and scattered in the air, some drops falling heavily upon the foliage about me. The ruffians lingered for a few seconds, and then, descending, tramped back towards the house. Hassan was avenged.

It was an impulse that actuated me, for until that moment I had hardly entertained a distant hope of saving Zoraka. But the notion took sudden hold on me, and no sooner were they melted into the darkness than I scrambled upon the wall, and cast a hasty glance downwards. The level of the bay was some three feet below me, and the black waters rolled and plunged against the wall with a sucking sound. Instantly I dived headlong into the depths. I had always been a strong swimmer, accustomed to long spells of endurance under water, but as the tide was high I had some misgivings in that black abyss whether I should succeed in struggling down to the floor of the sea. The current struck cool and heavy against my face; the darkness was profound, and all the noises of an inferno grated in my ears. I groped at a venture with both hands. . . . The pressure upon my brain tightened; I could hold my breath no longer; and I was throwing up my arms for a plunge towards the surface when my foot kicking in the vacancy struck upon something more solid. In a moment more I was clinging to the sacking with one hand, while with the other I fumbled for my knife. To this hour I have no definite remembrance of what followed. The intense weight upon my brain seemed to shove me deeper into the sea, while at the same time I was conscious of holding fast by the cords to keep myself from floating to the surface. My head was bursting; I felt strangled; if I had had my senses clear I am sure that I would have abandoned the desperate task. But the very numbness of my wits made me stick like a leech to the sacking. I can recall my fingers pressing upon human flesh, which yet seemed like nothing human. Visions of eyeless skulls floated through my mind. Whitened bones and monstrous evil fishes appeared to surround me. I had a dim sense of collision with some body which turned upon me and buffeted me. And then I knew no more until I was upon the surface of the waters, with the ringing of a thousand noises in my head, the light of stars and a calm moon, and something that lay dead and heavy across my arm.

Zoraka

Zoraka came to very slowly, as though her spirit obeyed its recall with reluctance. By this time the moon was vanishing over the city, and the grey mists of dawn were creeping over the bay. A spasm contracted her bosom, and she emitted a long thin breath; leisurely she opened her eyes and looked at me.

" Beloved! " she murmured faintly.

Her eyes dwelt languorously upon me, and with a gentle movement of her arms she reached for my neck.

" It is Paradise, then, " she whispered, and lay upon the sward, contemplating the dwindling stars of heaven with vague wistfulness. Kneeling I regarded her. Now that the circumstances had been rescued from tragedy a reaction rose in my mind. Something in Zoraka repelled me, something, it may be, derived from the association with that immutable smiling corpse. I could not wholly conceive her as a living woman; she seemed tainted and defiled of death, and by the embrace of that detestable body. I watched the dark beauty growing in her face, and the handsome suggestions of her dripping, white-robed figure with dispassionate curiosity, even with distaste. Her eyes shifted from point to point of the vault and drooped upon me; she sat up weakly, with a start, and clung suddenly to me, with a sigh.

"Star of my night," she said. "Thou wert with me even in death. Kiss me, my heart, kiss me."

I shrank away and softly loosened the hands upon my neck.

"Hush," I said, "this is no time for ill-considered passion. You have not been locked in the embrace of death. Pray rather to your God for peace."

She stared at me reproachfully. "What is this thou sayest?" she asked with pleading tenderness. "I have been in the arms of death ? Indeed, it is true. Surely I have knocked upon the gates of Paradise, and heard the wings of the houris. But now, behold, love, it is in thine arms I lie, and thou art my life. What has this touch of death mattered, since it has brought my life to me ? Listen, the bulbul sings in the laurels! Of what is he singing, beloved, save of thee and me ?"

She laid her head upon my shoulder, crooning softly like a child, but the chill and damp of her wet garments entered into my blood, and I shivered.

" Nay, offer up your prayers," I said, " to Mahomet and to Allah. Allah-il-allah! Shall one who has just come forth from the jaws of death through God's mercy turn upon Him and wrong His laws ? You are the wife of a man given under sacred ordinances. Are you a child that you should defy His goodness and challenge His loving kindness ?"

" A wife ? " she cried on a higher note. "I was sold into the bondage of the harem. Why may I not deliver myself ? I have been rejected and cast forth. I am dead. There, O Feringhi, lies poor Zoraka, the wife of Hassan, deep among the weeds and fishes of the sea."

" You deceive yourself with fond hopes," I answered. " The obligations of the world enwrap you still, like the chains upon a slave."

" I have broken them, I have derided them. Nought can bind me now," she cried proudly. She rose to her feet and tottering to me once more encircled me with her arms. " I love thee, Feringhi; yea, though it be a sin, and accursed of Allah, to desire a Giaour, I love thee, I desire thee; the heat of my passion burns in my body. See, it laps up these dripping garments. I lay my arm upon thy cheek. Mark how it is afire. Press upon my bosom, and feel the flame that consumes my heart. I am devoured with my love of thee. Of what account then are the pains and tribulations of hell with thee beside me ? Yea, though I forfeit Paradise and the favour of Allah, yet will I love thee and be thine.''

I shook my head. '' It is impossible,'' I said, '' I am a Feringhi from over the sea. My way lies apart. I am here for a moment of the sunshine, like the swallow. The meshes of your life enclose me. You and I may speak through the bars of a prison.''

She started from me. '' You do not love me,'' she cried fiercely. '' You would pass from me into the liberties of the world, and I must keep my prison ? Is this face not beautiful ? And yet it must fade and decay behind the veil. Have not the lines of my body moved you, and still must they wither in the shroud of these garments ? Must I lie all day within the harem walls, and must the song sing in my heart without an end ?

Oh my beloved!" and she threw herself upon me again. "I am thine and thou art mine. The Giaour is fashioned of stone; his heart is of marble; but it is stained and pierced with veins of blood. Thou lovest me and I love thee. Let us leave this place."

She spoke in a soft wailing voice, and though I had grown weary of her importunities and the clasp of her warm fingers gave me no thrill, I could not restrain a sense of pity in my soul. She was an outcast from the harem, accounted dead, and it seemed that I was the sole person left in her world. I was greatly perplexed, for it was plain that I could not leave her there, abandoned to the ruthless hand of Hassan. And yet I could conceive no means for her disposal. While I was deep in these awkward meditations, uppermost in which lay the necessity of an immediate departure, a low and quiet footfall sounded in the garden. Zoraka with her head upon my bosom heard nothing, but I, looking up, saw to my horror the burly form of Hassan approaching in the dim light. We stood in thick shadow, and he did not remark us, nor, indeed, do I think he was in any condition to do so. For he walked solemnly and slowly, as a man bent with sorrow, and mounted upon the little wall overlooking the bay without a glance upon either side. Here he remained for some moments motionless. The twilight of the dawn illumined his features indistinctly; the water, now grey and wan, washed with regular sounds against the wall. Hassan's eyes were troubled. The diabolic passion had vanished from his face, and it wore now even a patient melancholy dignity. Fearful, I held Zoraka closer to me, where she nestled without a word; but it was upon Hassan that my gaze was fixed. He stood silent, the breeze blowing his robes about, and then slowly bowing his head gave vent to

an inarticulate cry of great emotion. The
man's abasement touched me, and in the influence of his presence I was not aware that
Zoraka had raised her head and was looking
at me. Suddenly her arms relaxed about
me, and she followed the direction of my
glance. A short wailing scream broke from
her, and whirling giddily upon her feet, she
slipped and staggered into the open light.
At the noise Hassan turned quickly, and his
face changed rapidly; the expression upon
it wore swiftly round from wonder to terror,
and from terror to delight. He leaped from
the wall, and ran hastily towards her; and
in a second she was folded in his arms, and
he was caressing her with endearing tenderness. Zoraka stood silent, swaying upon
her feet, her eyes eloquent of fear and repulsion. He drew her closer, murmuring affectionately. It was plain that he had a passionate attachment to his unfaithful wife.

The interest of this scene held me spellbound, regardless of my own situation. It was not until Zoraka, folded helplessly in his embrace, turned her face towards me, that I recalled my own danger. I feared that she would call upon me, make some appeal to my love against this violation of her own person. Indeed her eyes, unseen of Hassan, fell upon me mutely, pleading and yearning, like the eyes of a beaten dog. She opened her lips, but no sound came. Hassan drew her gently with him down the sward, and her feet mechanically obeyed his impulse. Within my coign of shadow I watched them go, and, as she faded into the twilight of the morning, it seemed to me that once more she turned and implored me with those great and shining eyes.

V

En Route

JOHN CORFIELD reached Southampton very early. The boat was advertised to sail at ten o'clock, and close upon five empty hours lay still before him. And yet it was some relief to be here; in a way his spirit took new sensations from the idle, desultory air and the fresh liberty of exercise. In those last days London had come to crowd upon his courage. He breathed hard within those black walls; the dark skies confined him; the air of a prison surrounded him. There was the theatre of his folly and his crime, in which he was still a figure upon the stage. Westward and eastward, day by day, he must carry the private burden of his peril. The situation wore upon his nerve, and at last constrained him to flight. He was in a fret to depose these past and irremediable episodes from their proximity. The terror of suspense held him captive. And as the time of his departure approached this panic grew upon him into a fever. He urged the cab that took him to Waterloo into a faster pace; he stamped restlessly about the platform; he trembled with impatience for the guard's signal. But once at Southampton, and remote from the immediate centre of his troubles, he drew freer breath. The sea wind flew over the Water, cool and sweet; the town lay secure in its fine warm shelter. From the windows of the hotel he could watch far off the heavens darkling upon the Solent; a score of small sails were scattered upon the horizon; and in the distance, as the sun went down, a South African liner was tramping for the Heads. A little low, sad sound of water breaking upon stones rose from below and filled the rooms with murmur.

Corfield leaned forth of his window and inspired the strong flavour of the sea. He was a lithe, spare man, with a firm, wide jaw and sharp, fine eyes above a nest of deep lines. His fingers tapped upon the sill as he hummed very softly a plaintive Italian air. The details of the panorama pre-occupied him. The sun fell; the western sky flushed with gold; the Water flared with the shadow of the sunset; tiny sails, struck red as blood, gleamed from a dozen points about the harbour. Corfield watched the progress of this pageantry; swiftly the colours died, and slowly the pale, cold greys of the September night crept over the prospect, and slim, yellow points of light sprang up along the quays. His eyes wandered from the bleak water to the bright foreshore; the town hummed in his ears. He listened very idly. Far away upon a distant spit of land

a great flash rose and died.   It drew his in-
curious gaze.   A noise of hammering echoed
from the streets; voices lifted in laughter
and passed by.   The great silence of the
evening closed upon the port; the sea-wind
dropped; and only the little waves curling
on the pebbles below made a sound in his
ears.

Corfield withdrew his head, and shutting
the window, rang the bell.   "Let my
things be taken to the boat at nine," he said
to the waiter, "and give me some dinner in
this room at seven."

"Yes, Sir," said the man.   "Table
d'hote, Sir?"

Corfield paused a second.   "No," he
said, slowly.   "Bring me a menu and I'll
arrange the courses myself.   A wine list
too."

He turned again to the window and looked
forth.   The prospect lay dark and quiet, but
the desolation did not affect his compla-

cence. Upon the waiter's reappearance he examined the bill of fare with deliberate attention, ticking off the dishes with a pencil. "Bring me a magnum of No. 35," he said, curtly.

He looked at his watch, rose, and putting on his hat, descended the stairs. The town was in comfortable warmth and brightness; streams of passengers flowed along the footways; and the roads ran brisk with traffic. For an hour he strolled about the streets surveying the scenes with indolent interest, and then he returned to the hotel. He was met upon the staircase by the waiter, deferential and apologetic.

"A lady has called, Sir. She says you expect her. She is in your room."

Corfield started, his eyes contracted swiftly, and he moistened his lips. "Whom did she ask for?" he inquired.

"No one by name, Sir. She described you, and said you were sailing to-night."

"Very well," said Corfield; "that is right. I was expecting her."

He walked upstairs quietly, and opened the door of his room without hesitation.

"Well, Nina, it is you?" he said.

The woman turned quickly in her chair, the colour ran into her pale face suddenly, and with her joyous smile of welcome a dimple shone out upon either cheek.

"Oh, Jack!" she cried, "oh, Jack!"

She burst into tears and clung about him sobbing; the rich cloak dropped from her shoulders and fell to the floor. Corfield patted her head without emotion, and stooping, picked it from the ground.

"How did you find me?" he asked.

"George told me," she answered between her sobs; " I begged him. He knew he could trust me. Oh, why didn't you tell me?"

"He should not have told you," said Corfield, frowning. He stared at the floor reflectively. "Why have you come?"

She put her arms about him with a pretty motion. '' How can you ask ?'' she cried. '' Oh, Jack! how can you ask me such a question ? I am coming with you.''
Corfield examined her with care, scrutinising her stained face with cold curiosity. '' I think you do love me, Nina,'' he said at length. ''But do you understand what it means ? Women rarely understand.''

'' Oh, yes,'' said Nina, earnestly; '' you are a fugitive, I know. You must go abroad. I am going with you.''

'' I am a criminal,'' he said. '' To-morrow the town will be shouting for my blood. I have robbed hundreds of people. This escape of mine is a tacit confession. You see, it's no use making pretences. If you are to come with me, we must be frank.''

'' Yes, yes,'' she said, weeping afresh; '' I don't care what you are. I don't care for anything but you.''

" I cannot even marry you," said Corfield, thoughtfully.

She used a gesture of impatience. " Have I ever thought of that before ? " she asked.

" No; but this is a public matter," he said. " It stands upon another footing. Do you realise that to-morrow you will be in all the papers, a notorious woman, associated with a notorious thief ? "

He spoke brusquely, holding her at the length of his arm, his eyes studiously upon her face. She broke into a ripple of laughter, and the dimples ran into her cheeks again. She strove to reach him with her arms, but his grasp held her in a vice.

" Once more listen," he went on, in his slow, even tones. " Do not buoy yourself up with false sentiments about me. I am what I seem to be. See! " He left her, and crossing the room, touched with his foot a heavy box which lay in a corner.

"There are twenty thousand pounds here. I am a thief," he said, calmly.

Again she laughed; and following after, flung out her arms upon him, drawing his face to hers. "Jack! Jack!" she cried.

Corfield's eyes met hers, which besought him from their great deeps. He kissed her.

"Yes, you do love me, Nina," he said; "I always thought so."

He gently disengaged her fingers from his neck. "Sit down," he said, persuasively; "you must be very tired. Did you find it a dull journey? I hate trains myself; and there was a baby in my compartment. It got in at the last moment. They ought not to allow women in smoking carriages upon any emergency. Won't you sit? Oh, by the way, I've ordered dinner at seven, and it will be here immediately. I must tell them to lay for two."

His voice was placid; he spoke more deliberately than accorded with his use; and his face showed like a blank face in marble. It was cold and grey in colour. Only his eyes made any display of life, and it seemed to the woman that they moved and suffered behind a veil. There was no appearance of discomfort save in her own agitation, and for all the anxiety he wore they might well have been prepared and settled for an ordinary dinner in the sober round of the year. It was this very passivity of his manner that frightened her.

"Oh, don't Jack; don't be like this!" she entreated, catching his hand. "Be yourself. Tell me. Oh, speak to me properly! Oh, Jack, Jack, will they catch you?"

She ended with a gulp of emotion, hiding her face upon his breast.

"Nina, you are a goose," said he, lightly; "don't be silly. Of course, I don't expect them to catch me. Do you think I should be here, if I did? How am I to talk to you, if you're——? There, don't go off in a flurry. It was very good and sweet of you to come. Let me ring the bell."

She fluttered into a chair as the noise of the waiter came up the stairs, and, with her chin in one palm, stared without observation through the window.

"Ah, yes, that's a pretty view, isn't it?" said Corfield, with a glance at her and then to the waiter: "Lay for two, please. My wife will dine with me."

When the door had closed Nina rose to her feet and approached him swiftly with her arms out. Her eyes were full of tragedy, her attitude was designed for appeal. He anticipated the outbreak of tears and the tumultuous pleadings, and he winced.

"For heaven's sake don't make scenes, my dear girl!" he urged, meeting her on the way. "Come, you shall have a glass of wine now to put you right."

"No, no!" she cried; "I am all right. I——"

"Well, cry then, and get it over," he said, with a sigh of resignation. "There's a bedroom in there."

"Oh, for God's sake, pity me!" she broke forth.

Corfield stared at her, and then the wrinkles grew into bunches beneath his eyes, and his lips curled. The situation stirred a forgotten sense of humour in him.

"Well," said he, smiling, "and won't you pity me?"

Nina lifted her head from her hands sharply. She started as though quickened by a new idea. "Yes, yes," she said. "Oh, how selfish of me! I didn't look at it like that, Jack; believe me I didn't, or I would sooner have cut off my hand than worried you. Oh, my poor Jack! Yes, yes, I know—there's the waiter. I'll just run in the other room and wash my face."

She hurried away in confusion, and Corfield sat down to the table and picked up a paper. When she returned the dishes were set. Corfield looked up from his reading. " I sent the waiter away," he explained; " I thought you wouldn't want him here."

" No, no: thank you, Jack," she assented, hastily; and then, glancing at him, put out a finger and touched him timidly. " Have I spoiled myself crying ?" she asked, with a little laugh of embarrassment. " Won't you kiss me, Jack ?"

He looked up at the tall, slight figure that stood beside him; the grey eyes pleaded with him from the handsome face. They touched him for a moment with their memories; he put his arm round her suddenly. " Why, certainly," he said, softly; " you could never spoil your looks, Nina. You will be handsome in your grave."

She laughed gently and bent to his caress. " Oh, yes, in my grave !" she said, in mock reproach. " That might be to-night."

She hung over, smoothing his hair and

laying her cheek upon his shoulder. He moved slightly beneath her touch, and she withdrew and took her seat at the table. "And now, Jack," she said, gaily, "what are you going to give me?"

"Hors d'œuvres for a start," he answered; "and we must make the best of this champagne, such as it is. However, we'll manage, I daresay."

She laughed again and nodded with a manner of liveliness; but the laugh and the liveliness was too clearly dictated by a resolution. Corfield picked over the dishes with his fork, eating sparingly and maintaining a fluent conversation. He spoke of irrelevant matters—of the races at the Goodwood Meeting, of the newest play, of the great cause that was proceeding; and finally fixed his eyes upon her.

"That is a very pretty dress, Nina," he said. "Didn't I give you that? Yes; I thought so. I haven't bad taste. It suits your svelte figure." And he surveyed her critically.

Her pale face flushed and she smiled tremulously. "Jack, how you stare!" said she; and the next second her jaw fell and she gazed blankly at her plate; the colour receded, leaving her face wan and haggard. The courses passed untouched, she moved her fork upon them and laid it down. She heard Corfield talking in his smooth, soft voice, but had no sense of his words. It was like the sea grumbling upon the pebbles. Suddenly he looked up, and there was a silence of which she was vaguely conscious. She started and her glance met his.

"Nina," he said, sharply, "why don't you eat?" Her lips trembled as he held her eyes. She opened her mouth as if to speak, gaped, and was silent.

"Nina!" said Corfield.

"I can't," she stammered.

"Nonsense," he returned. "Drink your

wine, and don't be foolish. It will do you good."

"I—it would choke me," she gasped, with a sob.

Corfield frowned, but his voice was soft and grave as he answered:

"You must do as I tell you. We have a long journey. You must keep yourself up."

She glanced at him fearfully, and with a whimper set the glass to her lips. It rattled against her teeth. Corfield watched her, and then filling his own glass anew, put back his head and drank the wine at a gulp.

"There!" said he; "it's warming, and one needs warming to-night." The champagne stirred the pulse of his heart, and he smiled at her affectionately. "I'll ring for the next course. You must remember I've had no lunch."

"Oh, Jack!" she cried, spasmodically.

"I wonder how we shall fare to-night. I

don't think it will be rough. Are you a good sailor, Nina? I forget. However, there'll be plenty of time to get your legs. We mustn't moon, Nina. We must have a good time. You must be gay. Do you think you can ever be gay again?''

''Where are we going?'' she asked, breathlessly.

He laughed and drank again. '' That depends if we get there. Fill up your glass, child.''

'' Oh!'' she said, tersely, and fixing her troubled eyes on him, '' and you have lost so much. Everything is gone—your position, your reputation, your home, and your wife——''

'' You pity me that?'' he asked, lifting his eyebrows.

'' No, no; but men do. Everything is gone!'' she cried, passionately.

'' Well,'' he replied slowly, '' I have twenty thousand pounds—and you, I suppose; and I have escaped gaol. Do you mind a cigarette at this stage?"

"There's no chance of——," she inquired in a voice of terror.

He shrugged his shoulders and struck a match.

"Well, if they do, I'm not a fool, my dear. I have my plans. I have my—preparations. Let us have another course: there's a bird of some kind."

He got up and rang the bell as he spoke, and the woman rose with him.

"What do you mean, Jack?" she cried. "What are you hinting at? Preparations! My God! what do you mean? Jack! Jack!" He turned from the bell-rope and confronted her, placidly. "Ah!" she screamed, pointing a finger at the bulging pocket of his coat. "Ah, Jack! what is that? Give it up to me, Jack—do you hear?" she called fiercely, and threw herself upon him.

"Don't be a fool, Nina!" he said, a little

roughly, and strove to fling her off. But she clung to him the closer, wreathing her arms about him and fumbling at his breast.

"You shall give it to me," she cried, fighting with her fingers—"you shall, Jack! You coward! You——"

"Hush, Nina, hush! There's the waiter coming. Oh, damnation, take it then!" he cried, angrily, and pushing her from him took his seat at the table quickly.

The woman, clutching the revolver quickly in both hands, swayed and staggered across the room.

"Sit down, sit down!" said Corfield, sharply, as a rap sounded on the door. "Sit down and have some wine. Quick!"

Hiding the weapon in the bosom of her dress, she fell into her chair and put her face in her hands, trembling with emotion.

"Come in," said Corfield, in his suave voice. The door opened. Corfield paused with his glass half-way to his lips; his eyes measured the man; and then, concluding the movement of his hands with deliberation, he drank the champagne slowly. He set the empty glass upon the table. Nina's head was hidden in her hands.

"Ah! it's you," said Corfield, quietly. Nina lifted her face in wonder, and the man came a step forward.

"I hold a warrant for your arrest, Mr. Corfield," he said, in a level voice.

At the words a short sharp cry started from the woman; she rose, like a spectre, pallid and dishevelled from her struggle.

"What are you doing here?" she cried, facing the stranger. "Oh, my God, what are you——"

Her shivering jaw fell and she stared at him.

"Hush, Nina!" said Corfield, interposing softly. "Sit down. You will alarm the hotel. You are alone?" he inquired, politely of the man.

The fellow shook his head with a smile. "The job's too big for that, Mr. Corfield. But I thought you'd like it better this way. They think I'm a friend come to see you off; there's no bother in the hotel."

"Quite right," said Corfield, suavely. "Very considerate of you. Sit down, Mr. ——"

He lingered over the designation and interrogated the newcomer. The detective shook his head. "I'm afraid it's impossible, Sir. Better make up your mind. The sooner we get it over the better. I'm sorry to disturb you."

He spoke shortly, but with studious civility; lithe and alert, he watched Corfield with restless eyes.

"It's a fact that you do," said Corfield with a smile; "and the lady, as you see, is not very well. You might give me a few minutes, at any rate."

The detective glanced for a moment at

Nina, who, shrunk in her chair, was regarding him with wide eyes of fear.

"Sorry to put you about, Madam," he said, "but——"

"What have you got there?" interrupted Nina, with a shrill cry, stretching a tremulous hand towards his coat. "Take it away! Oh, take it away!"

The detective touched his pocket. "Oh, I don't think we need use 'em, Madam. Come, better take it easily. Mr. Corfield knows."

She broke out suddenly into a fit of laughter, lying back in her chair and shaking in all her body.

"Nina," said Corfield, smoothly, "your nerves are all on edge, poor girl. Let her compose herself a little," he said, turning on the officer. "I can't leave her like this."

The man hesitated. "Well," he said, presently, "we might spare a minute or two."

There was a momentary silence, through

which the rustling of the bay was heard, and then Corfield pushed the bottle towards him. "Have a glass while you wait," he said, persuasively. "You're a friend, you know."

He smiled pleasantly. Nina giggled softly to herself. The detective glanced at the champagne, then at his prisoner, and he too smiled.

"I don't mind, Sir," he said, and sat down to the table with his eyes upon Corfield. Corfield filled a glass with care. "How did you find me?" he asked.

The detective smiled more grimly. "It's a pity you let this lady here follow you," said he, lifting the glass to his mouth. Corfield turned his glance on Nina. Suddenly the laughter left her, and she rose to her feet, silent and motionless for a second. Then with a scream she rose and flung her arms about Corfield.

"Oh, Jack, Jack!" she cried. "Oh, my God! Oh, Jack, Jack!"

She fell a dead lump across Corfield's arms. The detective pushed back his chair and came round the table; his features advertised a certain compassion. Corfield's eyes flashed suddenly upon him and back again to Nina.

" Get some water, quick," he said, hastily; and he moved his champagne glass nearer as though for handy use. The detective sprang back and reached for the decanter. Corfield loosened his grip of the woman, and deftly slipped two fingers into his waistcoat pocket. . . .

When the man was at his side with the tumbler the wine was singing loudly in Corfield's glass. He sprinkled Nina's hands with water and set the tumbler to her teeth.

" You see," he said, " it would have been cruel to have left her like this. She is much affected, but will be better presently."

The detective nodded, but a frown col-

lected on his forehead. The circumstances
of the job distracted him. Corfield carefully
spread his burden on the floor and opened
her bodice.

"She is coming to," he said, after a
pause. "Sit down, please, for a moment,
and finish your glass. I am sorry you have
been interrupted."

As if to set an example, he lifted his own
glass, and gently and slowly drank the wine.
He wiped his moustache, and sat looking at
Nina's body. The officer was silent, but he
sipped his wine uneasily, keeping his furtive
eyes on Corfield.

"It's a bad case," he said, presently;
"but you played for a big game, Mr. Corfield."

"I've always done that, my friend," said
Corfield, still watching Nina.

The body stirred upon the carpet; the
eyes opened.

"Come, Nina," said Corfield. "Bet-

ter ?'' Stooping, he picked her up, and
carrying her to her chair settled her comfortably in the seat. '' Drink this,'' he said,
putting a glass to her lips. She drank mechanically, and, leaning back, stared upon
him. Then her eyes wandered to the detective, and remained upon his face, wide and
vacant.

'' Silly girl to faint,'' said Corfield, pat-
ting her cheek. He returned to his chair.
The detective rose.

'' We must go now, Mr. Corfield,'' he said.

Corfield bit his lip. '' Come,'' he said,
'' You have seen how ill she is. You can't
expect me to leave her just now. Give me
—four minutes.''

'' It's very unusual,'' muttered the man,
undecidedly.

'' The case is unusual,'' responded Corfield, with a little smile. '' Nina, are you
better ?''

She made no answer, but continued her

steadfast gaze upon the detective. He rose, and she rose with him. Corfield settled his elbows on the table and leaned his face in his hands.

" Come, sir," said the detective, briskly. Corfield made no sign. The man walked up and tapped him on the shoulder. " Come, Sir," he said, more sharply.

Corfield lifted his eyes apathetically; they moved vacantly across the detective's face, and then passed beyond. Suddenly he flinched and shivered; an expression of horror and surprise started into his face.

" Nina! Nina!" he gasped in a hoarse whisper.

The detective, startled by the tones, whirled rapidly upon his heels; a sharp report rang in the room, and he fell struggling in a heap upon the floor.

Nina stood with the smoking revolver, her eyes following the movements of the body in a shifting stare.

There was absolute silence upon the room for some moments. Then Corfield stirred in his chair and parted his lips. He strove to rise. "Nina!" he cried, in a remote whisper. The woman's eyes turned upon him and she started.

He shook his head. "Too late!" he cried, in that thin whisper. A laugh choked itself in his throat. He shut his eyes and opened them, tossing his head as though to keep his senses. His features were gathered into a deep grimace of thought. "Give it—give it to me!" he murmured, thrusting out a hand aimlessly. "They will think— for God's sake——"

His head dropped upon the table. The fixed look melted in the woman's eyes; terror gathered swiftly in its place; and, with a shriek of anguish, she leapt across the body, and, still holding the revolver, flung herself upon Corfield.

VI

A Resurrection

I

THE book slid gently from Gregory's fingers, and closed with a rustle upon the table. He was not conscious of the movement, for in a moment he was rapt among high and tender memories. The verses sang in the current of his blood, and pulsed to the beating of his arteries. They resounded from distant years with the full rhythm of an immediate echo. These instant reverberations in a heart long silent startled him with their unexpectedness. It was so long since he had provoked that pale wraith and image of his old passion. And now of a sudden his fibres were quick with a soft and melancholy yearning. With that passage in the poem, long since forgotten, the resurrection of this untimely ghost was charged with delicate and private meaning. His eyes fell again upon the closed volume, and he repeated the verses in a soothing whisper to himself.

He could see Dorothea's lips move to the phrases, her hand flutter unawares about her heart, according to a habit which had always affected him. He saw her bend and lean to touch him with her pretty air of assurance; soft fingers rested upon his arm. He sighed, and dropping slowly in his chair smiled very plaintively at his own fancies.

He was conscious of a certain penitence for the long omission of this memorial respect. The appeal of those lines allured him; he smarted and stung to reflect upon that oblivion in which so long she had been buried. Dorothea's eyes solicited him with

their soft radiance; they seemed to intercede
with him for an interval of silent communion. That ghostly visitant in his mind
tremulously pleaded her cause. Was it so
much, she seemed to urge, to snatch a little
space, a fragmentary hour, from out a life
dedicated to another, a meagre alms to that
poor soul he once had loved? It seemed
odd to him that the voice he once had heard
ring so clearly in those rooms had been so
persistently mute. The echoes of those familiar tones had died out with the years.
What brought them from the silent corners
at so irretrievable a time as this evening?
He had foregone his lealty. He sighed and
directed his glance upon the wall of his
study where hung a slight water-colour
sketch. It formed but a dash of colour,
with no discernible proportions of a woman,
but still a faithful transcription of the
model. Dorothea had stood and posed
for that dainty sketch, and she it was in a

manner that still inhabited the coarse cloth and looked forth upon him from blurred eyes. Gregory slowly unlocked a drawer in his bureau, and withdrew a photograph, carefully enwrapped between covers. He held it before him, scrutinising it with attention, and the light of the reading-lamp streamed thickly upon the face.

There was just such a look in those poor eyes as had fulfilled them many a time in life. She watched him with that grave patience that had so sweetly mingled with her pretty playfulness. The head to Gregory wore an aureole, in its stream of bright hair. As he regarded the picture from under the arch of his hand, the facts and tenants of that room lost their importunate reality. At a stroke the winter was gone, and across the budding English meadows he walked with Dorothea in the spring. It was not so very long ago, but the ten years had spanned a tragedy for him. Was it possible, he wondercd, that love should pass quite away, should change and commute like the fashions of a generation ? His eyes suffused. Ah no, he thought, not such a passionate whole love as theirs. He had not forgotten, only not remembered these six years. Somewhere under the sweet earth Dorothea's gracious heart throbbed to his pulses, her pleading eyes were lit with thoughts of him. The photograph dropped from his fingers, as the book had done, and the curtains swung in a mist before him. His memories provoked a warm and happy past; a sense, as it were, of physical pleasure filled him in the recollection of those fine days, now gathered into forgotten Time. The sadness of his reveries filled him with a positive delight. He sighed again, and his glance fell newly upon the picture. Reinformed by his sensitive imagination the bright flesh sparkled with life; the image reproached him with its immeasurable eyes. It seemed that those six years which sounded in his ears so desolately long, which had worn so wearily, inadequately marked his supreme sorrow. The grass was ancient over Dorothea in those six miserable years. The world might well attribute to him a remarkable fidelity. At nights he had sat and thought upon her, those long and terrible nights when her departure was fresh among his griefs, those sad nights, too, upon which it became something of a solace to recall and to remember and to weep. The devotion of his mourning spoke to his great love, and yet now that his old happiness and glory were vivid before him, he knew that not six years, not ten, but a lifetime should be the limit of his irreconciliation. The tears welled in his eyes; a short little sob shook him; his shaded eyes devoured the portrait; and then a knock fell on the door and a light voice broke upon him.

" May I come in, Frank ? Are you busy ? "

The speaker awaited no invitation, as if sure of her answer, but came forward briskly to the table, and placed a hand affectionately upon Gregory's shoulder. With a hasty motion he slipped the photograph between the covers of the blotting sheet before him.

" Marion ! " he said softly, and touched her fingers gently, looking towards the fire in abstraction.

The sudden contrast offered by this apparition took him aback, and for a full moment he was appalled at his own infidelity. Those ashes of the past burning brightly in his heart, he was newly affronted with the present. But the ache faded slowly, leaving in its place a sensation which he could not determine for pleasure or pain. His thoughts ranged vaguely over the enlarged area of the problem.

"You are thinking, dear?" asked his wife, smoothing his hair with a gentle hand.

There was something particularly caressing in her touch, which fitted with Gregory's mood. He looked up at her and smiled.

"Yes, child," he assented with a sigh.

"Aren't they happy thoughts?" she asked, bending quickly to him with an imperious suggestion of affection.

He indulged the sentiment in his blood. He was used to flow upon his emotions, and now the resumed loyalty to Dorothea in nowise jarred upon a present kindliness for the beautiful woman at his side. He patted her hand, and sought her face with a distant smile. As he did so the tenderness of her regard struck him. Her hair, the full form of her face, were as unlike Dorothea's as they might well be, but there returned to him sharply the nameless and indefinite resemblances which had first attracted him to

Marion. Was it merely that she inspected him with the same eyes of love, or was it some deeper community of spirit between the dead and the living that recalled this likeness? For the first time he realised quite clearly why he had married her. Turning with an abrupt movement in his chair, he held her with his melancholy gaze. The sudden act ruffled the papers on the desk, and the blotting-pad slipped and fell to the floor. With her usual impulsiveness Marion stooped and gathered the scattered papers, still clinging to his hand. He had not understood the misadventure, and her next words startled him.

" Who is this ? " she asked.

Gregory saw that she had the photograph in her hand. He thrust out his disengaged arm, and put his fingers on it.

" It is a—a friend," he murmured faintly. Her clutch resisted his; she surveyed the portrait slowly.

" What friend ? " she asked curiously, and glanced at him.

Something she perceived in him made her drop his hand, and scrutinise the photograph again.

" Who is it, Frank ? " she said, with a display of agitation.

He cleared his throat. Though to himself the situation presented no anomalies, he felt that this was no occasion for candour.

" Oh, a very old friend, who is dead," he said; and then, breaking the silence that followed, " let me have it, Marion; I'll put it away."

" No," she said, starting from him. " I know."

He seemed to catch something tragic in her tone, but he laughed a little, as though undisturbed. " I don't think you do," he said vaguely, " you never met her."

" So this is she," said Marion in a low voice, heedless of his interruption. She contemplated the picture in silence, and then with a bitter cry threw it from her. " If I had known," she moaned, " If I had only realised ! "

Gregory stirred uneasily. " Come, Marion," he said soothingly. She shook off his hand, and lifted her face. " Did you love that woman ? " she asked suddenly.

Her manner hardened him; it was ungenerous that she should reproach him.

" You know I was married before," he said coldly.

" Did you love her ? " she repeated.

Her demeanour put him in the wrong; it was as if she was inviting him to plead guilty that she might pronounce his sentence. He rose impatiently.

" I think we have discussed this enough," he observed.

" You will not answer me," she broke forth passionately; and then " yes," she assented, " quite enough "; and without a word further walked from the room, closing the door softly behind her.

Gregory was vaguely troubled. A confluence of emotions mingled in his mind. He resented the interruption upon his thoughts. The opposition of the two women did not appear to him incongruous. He had been willing enough to entertain them in company, the one as that revisiting memory, the other as the near associate of his life. He had a sense of irritation with Marion's jealousy which had thus disturbed the current of his great regret. He was not a man accustomed to confront vexatious problems, and wondered petulantly why he might not follow his own feelings without challenge. He walked to the fire and poked it in annoyance, and then, returning to his table, once more took up the photograph. The simplicity of that countenance was underanged; its regard dwelt upon him with changeless affection. He sighed. Dorothea, at least, kept her full heart, placid with the old accustomed passion. It pleased and soothed him to consider that here he might commune with her still, discharged from the gross accidents of life. His attachment to Marion did not conflict with his undying compassion for the forsaken companion of his youth. And now, again, his blood was spinning with thoughts of that one who had been wrapt these six years in the shroud of death. The flow of the old mood resumed in him, and softly replacing the picture in his drawer, he opened the long windows of his room and walked forth silently upon the lawn.

The wind was blowing through the garden, and the rain flew in gusts upon his face. He passed down the walks and entered the dark shrubbery. Here was an interval of silence in the savage night. The little arbour peered through the barren branches, seeming to beg his pity, thus abject to the desolation of the winds. He could see through the dull panes Dorothea's face pass and repass. Her large eyes beckoned to him. This spot was consecrated with recollections, and the horrid winter aspect made him shiver. It appeared to consist with the broken pieces of his life. He recognised now how tragic was the dissolution of the beautiful dream. Inside the house he had taken a warmer prospect; but here his heart turned cold insensibly. The shrieking in the branches and the driven rain, the rude turmoil of these barbarous elements, partook of a demonstration against him. Only here, and apart from the public spaces of the garden, lay a little private altar between him and the past. He wondered drearily how he could have married again, wondered with no judgment upon himself, but only with a caressing pity, with tears, with a pathetic sense of isolation.

He had grown into a very tender mood,

and once indoors again, went direct to his wife's room. In the dim light he could discern her stretched in abandonment upon the bed, and putting out his hand he touched her.

"Come, dear," he said gently.

He was very full of kindness, and had the desire to hold her to him, and to comfort her. The roaring rain and the wind accompanied his feelings. Marion moved convulsively and gave no answer.

"Come, dear," he repeated affectionately.

She broke out weeping, and he gathered her in his arms, hushing her as he would a child upon his knee. He was sure that his heart was buried with Dorothea, and it was his duty to console and soothe this poor girl with fraternal solicitude. Suddenly she sprang from him.

"No, no," she cried between her sobs; "your arms have been about *her; her* head has rested on you. Oh, my God, Frank!

A Resurrection

Why didn't you tell me? Why didn't I realise? You have given me nothing—I only have the remnants. You are divided between me and the dead."

" No, no, no," he urged softly; "you are overwrought; you are foolish, Marion. This is being morbid." He would not deny that re-arisen love. It had broken its grave, and come forth, and its arms were about him.

She clung to him; she whispered passionately in his ear: she pleaded with him to dishonour and annul that old affection so associated with memories. And slowly in the accession of her neighbourhood, and under the warm spell of her arms, the forlorn images which he had entertained in his fancy retreated. Her clasp stirred him; the grace of her slender body, abandoned to this agony of weeping, shook him; her face, superfluous with tears, invited his hesitant lips. He drew her closer, whispering to her questions.

"Yes, yes, you know I love you, dear," he murmured; "and you are first, darling, you are first."

Before this renunciation that freshly-awakened ghost withdrew, reluctant. She was denied her dignity; her attendance was discharged. Beneath the earth, where Dorothea's gracious heart had so long beat to his she must again seek the cold refuge of oblivion.

Marion put her hands about his neck, and the eyes that looked upon her were alight and shining.

II

As the sun struck through his window Gregory set down his pen and looked forth. It was odd, he reflected, that these thoughts pursued him at this particular stage in his life. The remembrance of his first wife had not fallen upon him since his re-marriage, until this trivial accident had provoked it.

And now she returned persistently. He was quite aware that the verses upon which he was engaged were inspired with the sentiments of that revival. He felt in his secret thoughts that it was impossible to forget. He was still loyal to his dead wife, and it was only in the actual mellay of daily life that the living interfered with her sovereignty. He hung now between the past and the present, with no embarrassment and with no mental confusion, but merely with alternate and comfortable changes of sentiment. Though Marion's nature was infinitely more emotional in reality, his own was wont to be more readily occluded by the drifts and shadows of spectral passions. She, upon her part, was for the time reconciled with her fears. He had confessed that she was first in his heart, and in the glory of that truth she was losing her pain at the knowledge that he had ever thought he cared for some one else.

" It was before he met me," she repeated to assure herself, " and he has never loved any one but me. . . . Men make mistakes " she told herself, " and he took pity upon her. . . . With that childish face, of course——;" and of a sudden the image of the woman that had forestalled her stabbed her like a knife.   But in the glow of her returning confidence she put the temptation from her heart.   And thus Gregory sat in his room composing his tender lyric to the dead, and his wife following her domestic charges about the house smiled at her foolish distrust.

But in truth these various moods were too delicate to endure, and the passionate nature of the woman was as perilous as the sentimental weakness of the man.

" Sing something, Marion," said Gregory in the evening.

She started, roused sharply from a temporary doubt that was darkening her thoughts.

“What shall I sing?” she asked unemotionally.

She wondered dismally if such a request had ever been presented before in that room, and the recurrence of that thought quickened her with sudden pain. She glanced at her husband, where he lay sunk within the comfortable arms of his chair, his own gaze vacant and wistful upon the fire.

“What is it you want?” she demanded in a sharper note.

He started. “Let us have—you play Chopin, don’t you, Marion? Play that waltz. You must know it. I think it’s 61.”

Marion’s hands fell rudely upon the keyboard. Like himself she was designed by her own emotions, with little interference of her reason; but what in him proceeded in weak sentimentality issued from her in loud passion. Her blood was resolutely gathering heat, and she was slowly graduating into a frenzy of anger. But Gregory sat by unconscious, floating upon the music along past reaches of his life. He stirred upon the conclusion, and lifted his chin with a sigh. At that, the woman broke forth on him.

"Why do you sigh?" she cried fiercely, turning swiftly upon her seat and confronting him. "What do you mean by treating me like that? How dare you? You coward! You're thinking—you're thinking —I know what you're thinking of. You cannot deny it. I defy you to deny it."

To his early start of surprise succeeded in Gregory's face a cold disapproval.

"I do not understand you," he said in a chilling voice. "You are singularly hysterical. I cannot pretend to follow you."

She laughed harshly, and struck the notes in a discord.

"Don't you? I have less difficulty in following you," she replied, with suppressed scorn. She played a bar or two. "I will not be used to recover your memories of the dead.''

A flush sprang in Gregory's cheeks. '' What do you mean ?'' he asked angrily.

'' You understand quite well,'' she replied with passionate deliberation, smoothing her cuffs with studied calm. '' It was an excellent thought to make me fill the place of that—that woman. Men must condescend to makeshifts and stopgaps. But now that I know, it is another matter. I have no intention of supporting the memory, or of filling the post of—what was her name, by the way ?'' she inquired with some exultation.

Gregory shuddered. He had been hurried into such rude and abrupt emotions. As he considered her, Marion appeared to him at this moment vulgar, clamant, almost as a shrieking shrew with hands to her hips. And he had been roused from a meditation of sorrowful sweetness to confront this. He had been moving freely among the tender memories of Dorothea, and the music had assisted his mood. This strident outbreak irritated him, and he frowned.

"You—you drive me beyond endurance," he cried, in a lower voice and with a gesture of despair.

Marion laughed. "Oh, I daresay," she said, being herself indeed under the stress of feelings that could find no issue in language. He rose, and the sound distracted her. She clutched him fiercely by the arm.

"It was true?" she asked, fixing him with her scornful eyes.

"What was true?" he asked, shifting his glance uneasily.

"You were thinking of—why, what was her name? I ought to have informed myself of that long ago."

She laughed hysterically. He shook off her hand; the woman was blatant, and deserved no consideration.

" It was true that I was thinking of past episodes in my life which were more pleasant than the present," he said slowly, and with the intention to hurt her.

She rose with a cry from her stool, and, with blazing eyes, confronted him a moment. Then, with a swift change, the whole aspect of her face was struck to despair. She sprang to him.

" Oh, my God! don't say that, Frank, don't say that. Oh, you will break my heart—you are killing me."

She broke into convulsive sobbing; a great, dull pain throbbed in her side. Mechanically he patted her.

" There, there," he said.

" Don't you see you are killing me ?" she murmured. " Oh, you don't know. You kill me. Oh, my God! I don't want to hear her name. Say, you lied, you lied. You did not think of her, did you—did you, Frank ?"

The desolation of that clinging figure touched him.

"No, no," he said soothingly, "no, no, dear. You—you are mistaken. But you aggravated me. You——"

"Yes, yes, forgive me," she pleaded. "I know it was only the piece itself affected you. We have both been melancholy to-day. Oh, Frank, Frank!"

Her arms encircled him; he was enclosed, as it were, within the greedy emotion of her love. Her face, moist with tears, entreated him with an imperious plea for affection. He bent and kissed her.

"I think we must not misunderstand each other, Marion," he said. She shifted her face against his with a little shudder.

"O darling," she sighed, "I am mad, I am mad. Of course I know. But you see, dear, it is this way. Now I know that you care for me, and never cared for her. It's bad enough like that, isn't it, dear Frank?

But we won't think of that. I am your only love. Men make mistakes; there are many fancies, but only one thing is real. Isn't that it?"

"Yes, dear, yes," he murmured tenderly.

He was engaged in the proximity of her beauty. He felt that he loved her. No shadow of the dead fell across that reconciliation.

"We will never think of it again," he whispered.

"Never, never," she murmured tenderly. "We will destroy all traces that might bring bitterness. Come," she cried, starting from him impulsively, "let us do so now."

"What do you mean, dear?" he asked softly.

"The—the photograph," she answered. "Let us burn all our misunderstandings with it."

She caught his hand, and the warmth of

her touch stirred him. He followed her from the room into his study.

Marion opened the drawer and withdrew the picture. She held it averted from her.

"Take it, dear, take it," she cried tremulously. She thrust it into Gregory's hand, and, still with his clasp in hers, he contemplated in silence the faded lineaments. A vague sense of pitifulness crept over him. The claims, embodied in that face, arose resurgent in his heart. Dorothea looked forth on him with the familiar eyes; but this unnatural conflict were best determined, this memory were best re-laid in its habitual grave. He moved towards the grate.

"Throw it in," urged Marion. He stood hesitant, the prey of discordant motives. "Frank! Frank!" she called pitifully.

With sudden movement of his fingers the card was jerked into the fire, and lay for a second intact upon the bright coal. He drew a long breath of pain; a sigh came from Marion also.

"Was she beautiful?" she asked, her hand covering her eyes.

He paid no heed to her question. Marion lifted her hand and pushed the poker into the coals; the flames leaped and lapped out the discoloured pasteboard.

"There, dear; see, we are burning our misunderstanding. You are mine; you have always been mine," she cried.

The stiff board slid forward and presented itself for a moment to Gregory's gaze. A black streak lay like a cruel tongue across the face.

"Poor girl! poor girl!" said Marion. She wrung her hands. "She was nobody—what has she to do with you or me? There burns a young friend of yours, Frank—a friend only."

Suddenly, and with an exclamation of horror, Gregory stooped low and snatched fiercely at the smouldering fragment.

"What you doing? Frank! Frank!" cried his wife in distress.

"Leave me alone," he said sharply, shaking off her hand.

"Do not touch it! Dare to touch it!" cried Marion, gasping.

He turned with the blackened paper in his hand, and his face was torn with emotion. She appeared to him like a brutal wanton, a devil that had tempted him to a cruel act. Ah, the pain of that sad, desolate heart beneath the grass!

"I will never forgive you all my life," he broke forth angrily. "You—you are a devil."

"Why—why——" she stammered, her mind tossing in the drift of her emotions.

"I loved her," he said furiously; "I loved her, do you hear? And you—you who attracted me by a chance resemblance, you——"

His passionate utterance went no further.

Her face had fallen ashen; she moistened her lips and then with a little meaningless motion of her hand, she stroked her hair.

" Let me go," she murmured, and walked uncertainly to the door.

The long windows of the dining-room stood open, and the moonlight was in flood upon the garden. Marion walked forth without intelligence of her action. Her dress trailed heavily upon the wet grass, and was snatched and plucked by the briars as she passed. Her brain was a heavy lump within her head; her heart, faint and tremulous, was shot at intervals with ominous pains. The calamity had fallen at the very moment of her triumph. She understood not that when she had merely dreaded she had not really suffered. Now that she realised, her frail world broke about her. His words had been a pitiless weapon against her, and she had fled as by instinct to hide the dishonour of her wounds in private, as some poor hunted creature steals away to die.

Marion stood near the gateway and looked out across the meadow. It seemed to her now that she had come into this house upon a false pretence; she had no rights in it. She compared dully her joyous entrance barely six months before, in the full tide of summer, with this ruthless and ignoble expulsion. Circumferenced with her humiliation she contemplated the ruins of her life with staring, tearless eyes. The dark vault of the night, scattered with stars and spread with moonlight, shone blue and clear above her. The earth under the white frost glittered and glowed with a cold radiance. The moon struck the face of the world to silver; the illumination of her sorrow lay around her. Marion's eyes travelled over the great meadow to the verge of the uplands, and to them appeared in that far distance Gregory's slight and elegant figure, with its loitering gait; she saw him raise his head; the pale face with its odd fleck of colour in either cheek, smiled upon her. ' He opened his arms. . . . The meadow waved with wheat, but the same moonlight visited that opulent field of gold as shone upon this white and arid stretch before her. She could not discern between these rival pictures, the cold purview, this pitiless outcast, and the clanging gates that opened on her Paradise that warm summer evening. She clung to the palings of the fence, her body taut, her vision straining to resume that sweet inveterate fancy. A physical pain dwelt persistently in her side.

The phantasmagoria dissolved into the inhospitable winds of night. She clapped her hands to her face and cried aloud. The agony of that irreclaimable remembrance mocked her. She left the gates and walked wearily through the copse. The bare, disparaged trees crowded upon her like curious, pitiful strangers, receiving her to a community of desolation.

"But they will awake," she cried. "The spring will bring them to life."

She sank upon her knees in the vacant summer-house. She realised now that what she had intended was impossible. She could not leave him; she dared not forego the sight of that false face. Poor, passionate heart!

"I am a coward," she thought, weeping. His eyes had encountered other eyes in affection; other lips had touched his lips with thrills of happiness. And she inherited but the shadow of a loyal love; it was with the rags of that strong passion that she was invested. It was hard that she should be the victim of that great fidelity. . . . Suddenly a great pain stung fiercely at her heart.

His outbreak left Gregory with a slight

feeling of remorse, instinctive with a gentle nature. That stricken face made him uneasy, and he turned at once to comfort himself for his cruelty.

" It was diabolical to make me do that," he argued, and in an instant the appeal of that burned and charred fragment diverted his pity. But most of all it was himself that he commiserated. He had compassion upon himself when he remembered how Dorothea would have winced under this shame. He had denied her, and must carry a heavy load of guilt upon his sacrilegious soul. He offered himself to the enjoyment of sorrow. The grave had not held its tenant; the disembodied ghost stole silently along the familiar corridors with a new face of reproach. Her features were marked with agony; he had invoked her from oblivion to discrown and disown her. The ruins of that picture made his heart ache. Her radiant flesh was scarred and whealed with his handiwork; it was as though he had struck her in her patience and her resignation. She had asked but a private corner of his heart, and he had refused her with contumely. He wept upon that dead despoiled face. The memories of that young love were bright and persistent. They dissuaded him from his constancy to the present. Now he thought upon it, every act and issue of his late life revolted him in his infidelity to Dorothea. Her voice sounded low and musical in the room; her hands turned the pages of her favourite volume. She sat against the fire and watched him with a sigh, unobtrusive, silent, a voiceless, motionless reproach. Gregory rose and thrust aside the curtains. Across the lawn she seemed to move in her cerements as she had moved six years ago, but now with a saddened step and downcast eyes. She paused by her rose-bush; she lingered in reluctance on her way. Opening the window he followed, in the unconscious pursuit of his melancholy fancy.

There, below the hollies, she might now be preceding him, as she had walked a thousand times in life. He entered the copse, and could imagine that she stopped and beckoned to him. His eyes fell upon the arbour. Surely it was thither that she would have him go, to commune there together as they had done so many summer evenings long ago. As he approached the summer-house a flash of wonder turned his heart to stone and then set it beating hard. From the high regions of his soaring fancy he fell suddenly to fact. He sprang forward with a cry of bewilderment; for Dorothea's face, white and immobile, peered through the dim and grimy panes at him. He pushed aside the ivy, trembling, and stood staring through the entrance. . . . Was it Dorothea's ? . . .

Upon that new grave he might now rear

a second temple to the dead, and from her quiet place among the shadows she too might now steal forth to revisit his melancholy dreams.

AT THE FIRST CORNER

By H. B. MARRIOTT WATSON

" We willingly bear witness to Mr. Watson's brilliance, versatility, and literary power. 'An Ordeal of Three' is a fancy that is full of beauty and delicate charm. When, again, Mr. Watson deals with the merely sordid and real side of East-end London he justifies his choice by a certain convincing realism which is never dull, and which is always inevitably true."—*Pall Mall Gazette*.

" A collection of nine stories admirably told by a master who has been much copied but never equalled. Mr. Marriott Watson has all the qualities of strength, imagination, and style, combined with a very complete sense of proportion."—*Vanity Fair*.

" Mr. Marriott Watson can write, and in these new stories he shows, more manifestly than in any previous work, his capacity for dramatic realisation. 'An Ordeal of Three' has not only strength but charm."—*Daily Chronicle*.

" Admirably conceived and brilliantly finished ; the book will be read."—*Saturday Review*.

" Knowledge of life, literary cleverness, charm, and above all, style, are present all through. One cannot dip into his volume without being taken captive and reading every story."—*Realm*.

" Remarkable for diversity of subject and distinction of style. Every page of this charming volume is original."

—*Black and White*.

" Mr. Watson can tell a story in a terse, vigorous, and thrilling manner."—*Westminster Gazette*.

" Contains the best work he has yet done. Uncommonly well written."—*Sketch*.

" There is undeniable power in the volume of stories, 'At the First Corner,' and there is something very like the fire of genius behind this power. The style is terse, vivid, and imaginative."

—*Guardian*.

" Exceedingly well written. There is no denying Mr. Marriott Watson's strength and delicacy of style."—*Queen*.

" There is an impressive ' grip ' in Mr. Watson's narrative from which the reader cannot easily escape."—*Whitehall Review*.

GALLOPING DICK

Being Episodes in the Life of Richard Ryder, sometime
Gentleman of the Road.

By H. B. MARRIOTT WATSON

" We have no hesitation in speaking of 'Galloping Dick' as a
distinct creation, as a new and wonderfully novel addition to that
select band of living individualities to which books are now the
only access."—*Saturday Review*.

" The book ennobles the literature of the highwayman. Dick
Ryder is perhaps the most delightful rascal of the road to be found
in the fiction that treats of his kind."—*Dundee Advertiser*.

" Men and women may read it with an assured anticipation of
enjoyment."—*Daily Chronicle*.

" He is an artist consummate and supreme . . .   The dialogue
which runs between them, the nicely-balanced sally and repartee,
the subtly-builded sentences, the proper arrangement of epithets,
the quaint affectation of the style and through all the fine flavour
and exhalations of the eighteenth century, are such that no lover
of literature can afford to miss."—*Pall Mall Gazette*.

" A magnificent example of the picaresque novel, which is like to
become the vogue once more. Dash and humour carry you from
page to page and you are not disappointed from first to last. It is
a triumph of writing."—*Black and White*.

" It is said that good wine needs no bush ; certainly 'Galloping
Dick' does not stand in much need of any one's recommendation."
                                        —*Literary World*.

" He is a most delightful cut-throat. We are sorry indeed to part
company with him, and should rejoice if he should at any future
time feel disposed to make a reappearance on the highway—of
literature."—*Sunday Times*.

" We have an always attractive theme worked up in an unpre-
tentious but thoroughly effective style."—*Daily Telegraph*.

" It is extraordinarily good. In a series of episodes, each of
which is complete in itself, it relates the amazing adventures of a
gentleman of the road."—*Westminster Gazette*.

" The author paints with many bold and characteristic touches
the loose morals, the wit, and unblushing speech of the men and
women of these audacious times."—*Daily News*.

" He is a gay rascal and for our introduction to him on his way
to the gallows we owe Mr. Watson our hearty thanks."—*Bookman*.

JOHN LANE, London and New York

JOHN LANE
THE BODLEY HEAD
VIGO ST
W.
Telegrams
"BODLEIAN
LONDON"
JOHN LANE THE BODLEY HEAD
JOHN LANE THE BODLEY HEAD VIGO STREET
E NEW
CATALOGUE of PUBLICATIONS in BELLES LETTRES

List of Books

IN

BELLES LETTRES

Published by John Lane

The Bodley Head

VIGO STREET, LONDON, W.

Adams (Francis).
ESSAYS IN MODERNITY. Crown 8vo. 5s. net. [*Shortly.*
A CHILD OF THE AGE. Crown 8vo. 3s. 6d. net.

A. E.
HOMEWARD: SONGS BY THE WAY. Sq. 16mo, wrappers, 1s. 6d. net. [*Second Edition.*
THE EARTH BREATH, AND OTHER POEMS. Sq. 16mo. 3s. 6d. net.

Aldrich (T. B.).
LATER LYRICS. Sm. fcap. 8vo. 2s. 6d. net.

Allen (Grant).
THE LOWER SLOPES : A Volume of Verse. Crown 8vo. 5s. net.
THE WOMAN WHO DID. Crown 8vo. 3s. 6d. net. [*Twenty-third Edition.*
THE BRITISH BARBARIANS. Crown 8vo. 3s. 6d. net. [*Second Edition.*

Atherton (Gertrude).
PATIENCE SPARHAWK AND HER TIMES. Crown 8vo. 6s. [*Third Edition.*
THE CALIFORNIANS. Crown 8vo. 6s. [*Shortly.*

Bailey (John C.).
ENGLISH ELEGIES. Crown 8vo. 5s. net. [*In preparation.*

Balfour (Marie Clothilde).
MARIS STELLA. Crown 8vo. 3s. 6d. net.
SONGS FROM A CORNER OF FRANCE. [*In preparation.*

Beeching (Rev. H. C.).
IN A GARDEN : Poems. Crown 8vo. 5s. net.
ST. AUGUSTINE AT OSTIA. Crown 8vo, wrappers. 1s. net.

Beerbohm (Max).
THE WORKS OF MAX BEERBOHM. With a Bibliography by JOHN LANE. Sq. 16mo. 4s. 6d. net.
THE HAPPY HYPOCRITE. Sq. 16mo. 1s. net. [*Third Edition.*

Bennett (E. A.).
A MAN FROM THE NORTH. Crown 8vo. 3s. 6d.
JOURNALISM FOR WOMEN : A Practical Guide. Sq. 16mo. 2s. 6d. net.

Benson (Arthur Christopher).
LYRICS. Fcap. 8vo, buckram. 5s. net.
LORD VYET AND OTHER POEMS. Fcap. 8vo. 3s. 6d. net.

Bridges (Robert).
SUPPRESSED CHAPTERS AND OTHER BOOKISHNESS. Crown 8vo. 3s. 6d. net. [*Second Edition.*

Brotherton (Mary).
ROSEMARY FOR REMEMBRANCE. Fcap. 8vo. 3s. 6d. net.

Brown (Vincent)
MY BROTHER. Sq. 16mo. 2s. net.
ORDEAL BY COMPASSION. Crown 8vo. 3s. 6d. [*Shortly.*
TWO IN CAPTIVITY. Crown 8vo. 3s. 6d. [*In preparation.*

Bourne (George).
A YEAR'S EXILE. Crown 8vo. 3s. 6d.

Buchan (John).
SCHOLAR GIPSIES. With 7 full-page Etchings by D. Y. CAMERON. Crown 8vo. 5s. net.
[*Second Edition.*
MUSA PISCATRIX. With 6 Etchings by E. PHILIP PIMLOTT. Crown 8vo. 5s. net.
GREY WEATHER. Crown 8vo. 5s. [*In preparation,*
JOHN BURNET OF BARNS. A Romance. Crown 8vo. 6s.
[*In preparation.*

Campbell (Gerald).
THE JONESES AND THE ASTERISKS. A Story in Monologue. 6 Illustrations by F. H. TOWNSEND. Fcap. 8vo, 3s. 6d. net.
[*Second Edition.*

Case (Robert H.).
ENGLISH EPITHALAMIES. Crown 8vo, 5s. net.

Castle (Mrs. Egerton).
MY LITTLE LADY ANNE. Sq. 16mo, 2s. net.

Chapman (Elizabeth Rachel)
MARRIAGE QUESTIONS IN MODERN FICTION. Crown 8vo, 3s. 6d. net.

Charles (Joseph F.).
THE DUKE OF LINDEN. Crown 8vo, 5s. [*In preparation.*

Cobb (Thomas).
CARPET COURTSHIP. Crown 8vo, 3s. 6d.
MR. PASSINGHAM. Crown 8vo, 3s. 6d. [*In preparation.*

Coleridge (Ernest Hartley).
POEMS. 3s. 6d. net.
[*In preparation.*

Corvo (Baron).
STORIES TOTO TOLD ME. Square 16mo, 1s. net.

Crane (Walter).
TOY BOOKS. Re-issue of.
This LITTLE PIG'S PICTURE BOOK, containing:
   I. THIS LITTLE PIG.
   II. THE FAIRY SHIP.
   III. KING LUCKIEBOY'S PARTY.
MOTHER HUBBARD'S PICTURE-BOOK, containing:
   IV. MOTHER HUBBARD.
   V. THE THREE BEARS.
   VI. THE ABSURD A. B. C.

Crane (Walter)—*continued*.
CINDERELLA'S PICTURE BOOK, containing:
   VII. CINDERELLA.
   VIII. PUSS IN BOOTS.
   IX. VALENTINE AND ORSON.
Each Picture-Book containing three Toy Books, complete with end papers and covers, together with collective titles, end-papers, decorative cloth cover, and newly written Preface by WALTER CRANE, 4s. 6d. The Nine Parts as above may be had separately at 1s. each.

Crackanthorpe (Hubert).
VIGNETTES. A Miniature Journal of Whim and Sentiment. Fcap. 8vo, boards. 2s. 6d. net.

Craig (R. Manifold).
THE SACRIFICE OF FOOLS. Crown 8vo, 6s.

Crosse (Victoria).
THE WOMAN WHO DIDN'T. Crown 8vo, 3s. 6d. net.
[*Third Edition.*

Custance (Olive).
OPALS: Poems. Fcap. 8vo. 3s. 6d. net.

Croskey (Julian).
MAX. Crown 8vo. 6s.
[*Second Edition.*

Dalmon (C. W.).
SONG FAVOURS. Sq. 16mo. 3s. 6d. net.

D'Arcy (Ella).
MONOCHROMES. Crown 8vo. 3s. 6d. net.
THE BISHOP'S DILEMMA. Crown 8vo. 3s. 6d.
MODERN INSTANCES. Crown 8vo. 3s. 6d. [*In preparation.*

Dawe (W. Carlton).
YELLOW AND WHITE. Crown 8vo. 3s. 6d. net.
KAKEMONOS. Crown 8vo. 3s. 6d. net.

Dawson (A. J.)
MERE SENTIMENT. Crown 8vo. 3s. 6d. net.
MIDDLE GREYNESS. Crown 8vo. 6s.

Davidson (John).
PLAYS: An Unhistorical Pastoral; A Romantic Farce; Bruce, a Chronicle Play; Smith, a Tragic Farce; Scaramouch in Naxos, a Pantomime. Small 4to. 7s. 6d. net.

Davidson (John)—*continued.*
FLEET STREET ECLOGUES. Fcap. 8vo, buckram. 4s. 6d. net.
[*Third Edition.*
FLEET STREET ECLOGUES. 2nd Series. Fcap. 8vo, buckram. 4s. 6d. net. [*Second Edition.*
A RANDOM ITINERARY. Fcap. 8vo, 5s. net.
BALLADS AND SONGS. Fcap. 8vo, 5s. net. [*Fourth Edition.*
NEW BALLADS. Fcap. 8vo, 4s. 6d. net. [*Second Edition.*
GODFRIDA. A Play. Fcap. 8vo, 5s. net.

De Lyrienne (Richard).
THE QUEST OF THE GILT-EDGED GIRL. Sq. 16mo. 1s. net.

De Tabley (Lord).
POEMS, DRAMATIC AND LYRICAL. By JOHN LEICESTER WARREN (Lord de Tabley). Five Illustrations and Cover by C. S. RICKETTS. Crown 8vo. 7s. 6d. net. [*Third Edition.*
POEMS, DRAMATIC AND LYRICAL. Second Series. Crown 8vo. 5s. net.

Devereux (Roy).
THE ASCENT OF WOMAN. Crown 8vo. 3s. 6d. net.

Dick (Chas. Hill).
ENGLISH SATIRES. Crown 8vo. 5s. net. [*In preparation.*

Dix (Gertrude).
THE GIRL FROM THE FARM. Crown 8vo. 3s. 6d. net. [*Second Edition.*

Dostoievsky (F.).
POOR FOLK. Translated from the Russian by LENA MILMAN. With a Preface by GEORGE MOORE. Crown 8vo. 3s. 6d. net.

Dowie (Menie Muriel).
SOME WHIMS OF FATE. Post 8vo. 2s. 6d. net.

Duer (Caroline, and Alice).
POEMS. Fcap. 8vo. 3s. 6d. net.

Egerton (George)
KEYNOTES. Crown 8vo. 3s. 6d. net. [*Eighth Edition.*
DISCORDS. Crown 8vo. 3s. 6d. net. [*Fifth Edition.*
SYMPHONIES. Crown 8vo. 6s. [*Second Edition.*
FANTASIAS. Crown 8vo. 3s. 6d.
THE HAZARD OF THE ILL. Crown 8vo. 6s. [*In preparation.*

Eglinton (John).
TWO ESSAYS ON THE REMNANT. Post 8vo, wrappers. 1s. 6d. net. [*Second Edition.*

Farr (Florence).
THE DANCING FAUN. Crown 8vo. 3s. 6d. net.

Fea (Allan).
THE FLIGHT OF THE KING: A full, true, and particular account of the escape of His Most Sacred Majesty King Charles II. after the Battle of Worcester, with Sixteen Portraits in Photogravure and over 100 other Illustrations. Demy 8vo. 21s. net.

Field (Eugene).
THE LOVE AFFAIRS OF A BIBLIOMANIAC. Post 8vo. 3s. 6d. net.
LULLABY LAND: Songs of Childhood. Edited, with Introduction, by KENNETH GRAHAME. With 200 Illustrations by CHAS. ROBINSON. Uncut or gilt edges. Crown 8vo. 6s.

Fifth (George).
THE MARTYR'S BIBLE. Crown 8vo. 6s. [*Shortly.*

Fleming (George).
FOR PLAIN WOMEN ONLY. Fcap. 8vo. 3s. 6d. net.

Flowerdew (Herbert).
A CELIBATE'S WIFE. Crown 8vo. 6s. [*Shortly.*

Fletcher (J. S.).
THE WONDERFUL WAPENTAKE. By "A SON OF THE SOIL." With 18 Full-page Illustrations by J. A. SYMINGTON. Crown 8vo. 5s. 6d. net.
LIFE IN ARCADIA. With 20 Illustrations by PATTEN WILSON. Crown 8vo. 5s. net.
GOD'S FAILURES. Crown 8vo. 3s. 6d. net.
BALLADS OF REVOLT. Sq. 32mo. 2s. 6d. net.
THE MAKING OF MATTHIAS. With 40 Illustrations and Decorations by LUCY KEMP-WELCH. Crown 8vo. 5s.

Ford, (James L.).
THE LITERARY SHOP, AND OTHER TALES. Fcap. 8vo. 3s. 6d. net.

Frederic (Harold).
MARCH HARES. Crown 8vo. 3s. 6d.
net. [*Third Edition.*
MRS. ALBERT GRUNDY : OBSERVA-
TIONS IN PHILISTIA. Fcap. 8vo.
3s. 6d. net. [*Second Edition.*

Fuller (H. B.).
THE PUPPET BOOTH. Twelve Plays.
Crown 8vo. 4s. 6d. net.

Gale (Norman).
ORCHARD SONGS. Fcap. 8vo. 5s. net.

Garnett (Richard).
POEMS. Crown 8vo. 5s. net.
DANTE, PETRARCH, CAMOENS,
cxxiv Sonnets, rendered in English. Crown 8vo. 5s. net.

Geary (Sir Nevill).
A LAWYER'S WIFE. Crown 8vo.
6s. [*Second Edition.*

Gibson (Charles Dana).
DRAWINGS: Eighty-Five Large Car-
toons. Oblong Folio. 20s.
PICTURES OF PEOPLE. Eighty-Five
Large Cartoons. Oblong folio. 20s.
LONDON : AS SEEN BY C. D. GIBSON.
Text and Illustrations. Large
folio, 12 × 18 inches. 20s.
THE PEOPLE OF DICKENS. Six
Large Photogravures. Proof Im-
pressions from Plates, in a Port-
folio. 20s.

Gilbert (Henry).
OF NECESSITY. Crown 8vo. 5s.
[*Shortly.*

Gilliat-Smith (E.)
SONGS FROM PRUDENTIUS. Pott
4to. 5s. net.

Gleig (Charles)
WHEN ALL MEN STARVE. Crown
8vo. 3s. 6d.
THE EDGE OF HONESTY. Crown
8vo. 6s. [*In preparation.*

Gosse (Edmund).
THE LETTERS OF THOMAS LOVELL
BEDDOES. Now first edited. Pott
8vo. 5s. net.

Grahame (Kenneth).
PAGAN PAPERS. Crown 8vo. 3s. 6d.
net.
[*New Edition ready immediately.*
THE GOLDEN AGE. Crown 8vo.
3s. 6d. net. [*Eighth Edition.*
A NEW VOLUME OF ESSAYS.
[*In preparation.*
See EUGENE FIELD'S LULLABY LAND.

Greene (G. A.).
ITALIAN LYRISTS OF TO-DAY.
Translations in the original metres
from about thirty-five living Italian
poets, with bibliographical and
biographical notes. Crown 8vo.
5s. net. [*Second Edition.*

Greenwood (Frederick).
IMAGINATION IN DREAMS. Crown
8vo. 5s. net.

Grimshaw (Beatrice Ethel).
BROKEN AWAY. Crown 8vo. 3s. 6d.
net.

Hake (T. Gordon).
A SELECTION FROM HIS POEMS.
Edited by Mrs. MEYNELL. With
a Portrait after D. G. ROSSETTI.
Crown 8vo. 5s. net.

Hansson (Laura M.).
MODERN WOMEN. An English
rendering of "DAS BUCH DER
FRAUEN" by HERMIONE RAMS-
DEN. Subjects : Sonia Kovalev-
sky, George Egerton, Eleanora
Duse, Amalie Skram, Marie Bash-
kirtseff, A. Ch. Edgren Leffler.
Crown 8vo. 3s. 6d. net.

Hansson (Ola).
YOUNG OFEG'S DITTIES. A Translation from the Swedish. By
GEORGE EGERTON. Crown 8vo.
3s. 6d. net.

Harland (Henry).
GREY ROSES. Crown 8vo, 3s. 6d.
net.
COMEDIES AND ERRORS. Crown
8vo. 6s.

Hay (Colonel John).
POEMS INCLUDING "THE PIKE
COUNTY BALLADS" (Author's
Edition), with Portrait of the
Author. Crown 8vo. 4s. 6d. net.
CASTILIAN DAYS. Crown 8vo.
4s. 6d. net.
SPEECH AT THE UNVEILING OF THE
BUST OF SIR WALTER SCOTT IN
WESTMINSTER ABBEY. With a
Drawing of the Bust. Sq. 16mo.
1s. net.

Hayes (Alfred).
THE VALE OF ARDEN AND OTHER
POEMS. Fcap. 8vo. 3s. 6d. net

Hazlitt (William).

LIBER AMORIS; OR, THE NEW PYGMALION. Edited, with an Introduction, by RICHARD LE GALLIENNE. To which is added an exact transcript of the original MS., Mrs. Hazlitt's Diary in Scotland, and letters never before published. Portrait after BEWICK, and fac-simile letters. 400 Copies only. 4to, 364 pp., buckram. 21s. net.

Heinemann (William).

THE FIRST STEP; A Dramatic Moment. Small 4to. 3s. 6d. net.
SUMMER MOTHS: A Play. Sm. 4to. 3s. 6d. net.

Henniker (Florence).

IN SCARLET AND GREY. (With THE SPECTRE OF THE REAL by FLORENCE HENNIKER and THOMAS HARDY.) Crown 8vo. 3s. 6d. net.   [Second Edition.

Hickson (Mrs. Murray).

SHADOWS OF LIFE. Post 8vo. 3s. 6d.   [Shortly.

Hopper (Nora).

BALLADS IN PROSE. Sm. 4to. 6s.
UNDER QUICKEN BOUGHS. Crown 8vo. 5s. net.

Housman (Clemence).

THE WERE WOLF. With 6 Illustrations by LAURENCE HOUSMAN. Sq. 16mo. 3s. 6d. net.

Housman (Laurence).

GREEN ARRAS: Poems. With 6 Illustrations, Title-page, Cover Design, and End Papers by the Author. Crown 8vo. 5s. net.
GODS AND THEIR MAKERS. CROWN 8vo, 3s. 6d. net.

Irving (Laurence).

GODEFROI AND YOLANDE: A Play. Sm. 4to. 3s. 6d. net.

Jalland (G. H.)

THE SPORTING ADVENTURES OF MR. POPPLE. Coloured Plates. Oblong 4to, 14 × 10 inches. 6s.
[In preparation.

James (W. P.)

ROMANTIC PROFESSIONS: A Volume of Essays. Crown 8vo. 5s. net.

Johnson (Lionel).

THE ART OF THOMAS HARDY: Six Essays. With Etched Portrait by WM. STRANG, and Bibliography by JOHN LANE. Crown 8vo. 5s. 6d. net.   [Second Edition.

Johnson (Pauline).

WHITE WAMPUM: Poems. Crown 8vo. 5s. net.

Johnstone (C. E.).

BALLADS OF BOY AND BEAK. Sq. 32mo. 2s. net.

Kemble (E. W.)

KEMBLE'S COONS. 30 Drawings of Coloured Children and Southern Scenes. Oblong 4to. 6s.

King (K. Douglas).

THE CHILD WHO WILL NEVER GROW OLD. Crown 8vo. 5s.

King (Maud Egerton).

ROUND ABOUT A BRIGHTON COACH OFFICE. With over 30 Illustrations by LUCY KEMP-WELCH. Crown 8vo. 5s. net.

Lander (Harry).

WEIGHED IN THE BALANCE Crown 8vo. 6s.

The Lark.

BOOK THE FIRST. Containing Nos. 1 to 12.
BOOK THE SECOND. Containing Nos. 13 to 24. With numerous Illustrations by GELETT BURGESS and Others. Small 4to. 25s. net. the set.   [All published.

Leather (R. K.).

VERSES. 250 copies. Fcap. 8vo. 3s. net.

Lefroy (Edward Cracroft).

POEMS. With a Memoir by W. A. GILL, and a reprint of Mr. J. A. SYMONDS' Critical Essay on "Echoes from Theocritus." Cr. 8vo. Photogravure Portrait. 5s. net.

Le Gallienne (Richard).

PROSE FANCIES. With Portrait of the Author by WILSON STEER. Crown 8vo. 5s. net.
[Fourth Edition.
THE BOOK BILLS OF NARCISSUS. An Account rendered by RICHARD LE GALLIENNE. With a Frontis-piece. Crown 8vo. 3s. 6d. net.
[Third Edition.

Le Gallienne (Richard)—
continued.

ROBERT LOUIS STEVENSON, AN ELEGY, AND OTHER POEMS, MAINLY PERSONAL. Crown 8vo. 4s. 6d. net.

ENGLISH POEMS. Crown 8vo. 4s. 6d. net.
[Fourth Edition, revised.

GEORGE MEREDITH: Some Characteristics. With a Bibliography (much enlarged) by JOHN LANE, portrait, &c. Crown 8vo. 5s. 6d. net. *[Fourth Edition.*

THE RELIGION OF A LITERARY MAN. Crown 8vo. 3s. 6d. net.
[Fifth Thousand.

RETROSPECTIVE REVIEWS, A LITERARY LOG, 1891-1895. 2 vols. Crown 8vo. 9s. net.

PROSE FANCIES. (Second Series). Crown 8vo. 5s. net.

THE QUEST OF THE GOLDEN GIRL. Crown 8vo. 6s. [*Fifth Edition.*

THE ROMANCE OF ZION CHAPEL. Crown 8vo. 6s.

LOVE IN LONDON: Poems. Crown 8vo. 4s. 6d. net. [*In preparation.*

See also HAZLITT, WALTON and COTTON.

Legge (A. E. J.).
MUTINEERS. Crown 8vo. 6s.
[Shortly.

Linden (Annie).
GOLD. A Dutch Indian story. Crown 8vo. 3s. 6d. net.

Lipsett (Caldwell).
WHERE THE ATLANTIC MEETS THE LAND. Crown 8vo. 3s. 6d. net.

Locke (W. J.).
DERELICTS. Crown 8vo. 6s.
[Second Edition.

Lowry (H. D.).
MAKE BELIEVE. Illustrated by CHARLES ROBINSON. Crown 8vo, gilt edges or uncut. 6s.

WOMEN'S TRAGEDIES. Crown 8vo. 3s. 6d. net.

THE HAPPY EXILE. With 6 Etchings by E. PHILIP PIMLOTT. Crown 8vo. 6s.

Lucas (Winifred).
UNITS: Poems. Fcap. 8vo. 3s. 6d. net.

Lynch (Hannah).
THE GREAT GALEOTO AND FOLLY OR SAINTLINESS. Two Plays, from the Spanish of José ECHEGARAY, with an Introduction. Small 4to. 5s. 6d. net.

McChesney (Dora Greenwell).
BEATRIX INFELIX. A Summer Tragedy in Rome. Crown 8vo. 3s. 6d.

Macgregor (Barrington).
KING LONGBEARD. With over 100 Illustrations by CHARLES ROBINSON. Small 4to. 6s.

Machen (Arthur).
THE GREAT GOD PAN AND THE INMOST LIGHT. Crown 8vo. 3s. 6d. net. [*Second Edition.*

THE THREE IMPOSTORS. Crown 8vo. 3s. 6d. net.

Macleod (Fiona).
THE MOUNTAIN LOVERS. Crown 8vo. 3s. 6d. net.

Makower (Stanley V.).
THE MIRROR OF MUSIC. Crown 8vo. 3s. 6d. net.

CECILIA. Crown 8vo. 5s.

Mangan (James Clarence).
SELECTED POEMS. With a Biographical and Critical Preface by LOUISE IMOGEN GUINEY. Crown 8vo. 5s. net.

Mathew (Frank).
THE WOOD OF THE BRAMBLES. Crown 8vo. 6s.

A CHILD IN THE TEMPLE. Crown 8vo. 3s. 6d.

THE SPANISH WINE. Crown 8vo. 3s. 6d.

AT THE RISING OF THE MOON. Crown 8vo. 3s. 6d.

Marzials (Theo.).
THE GALLERY OF PIGEONS AND OTHER POEMS. Post 8vo. 4s. 6d. net.

Meredith (George).
THE FIRST PUBLISHED PORTRAIT OF THIS AUTHOR, engraved on the wood by W. BISCOMBE GARDNER, after the painting by G. F. WATTS. Proof copies on Japanese vellum, signed by painter and engraver. £1 1s. net.

Meynell (Mrs.).
POEMS. Fcap. 8vo. 3s. 6d. net.
[Sixth Edition.
THE RHYTHM OF LIFE AND OTHER ESSAYS. Fcap. 8vo. 3s. 6d. net.
[Sixth Edition.
THE COLOUR OF LIFE AND OTHER ESSAYS. Fcap. 8vo. 3s. 6d. net. *[Fifth Edition.*
THE CHILDREN. Fcap. 8vo. 3s. 6d. net. *[Second Edition.*

Miller (Joaquin).
THE BUILDING OF THE CITY BEAUTIFUL. Fcap. 8vo. With a Decorated Cover. 5s. net.

Milman (Helen).
IN THE GARDEN OF PEACE. With 24 Illustrations by EDMUND H. NEW. Crown 8vo. 5s. net.
[Second Edition.

Money-Coutts (F. B.).
POEMS. Crown 8vo. 3s. 6d. net.
THE REVELATION OF ST. LOVE THE DIVINE. Sq. 16mo. 3s. 6d. net.

Monkhouse (Allan).
BOOKS AND PLAYS: A Volume of Essays on Meredith, Borrow, Ibsen, and others. Crown 8vo. 5s. net.
A DELIVERANCE. Crown 8vo. 5s. *[In preparation.*

Nesbit (E.).
A POMANDER OF VERSE. Crown 8vo. 5s. net.
IN HOMESPUN. Crown 8vo. 3s. 6d. net.

Nettleship (J. T.).
ROBERT BROWNING: Essays and Thoughts. Portrait. Crown 8vo. 5s. 6d. net. *[Third Edition.*

Nicholson (Claud).
UGLY IDOL. Crown 8vo. 3s. 6d. net.

Noble (Jas. Ashcroft).
THE SONNET IN ENGLAND AND OTHER ESSAYS. Crown 8vo. 5s. net.

Oppenheim (M.).
A HISTORY OF THE ADMINISTRATION OF THE ROYAL NAVY, and of Merchant Shipping in relation to the Navy from MDIX to MDCLX, with an introduction treating of the earlier period. With Illustrations. Demy 8vo. 15s. net.

Orred (Meta).
GLAMOUR. Crown 8vo. 6s.

O'Shaughnessy (Arthur).
HIS LIFE AND HIS WORK. With Selections from his Poems. By LOUISE CHANDLER MOULTON. Portrait and Cover Design. Fcap. 8vo. 5s. net.

Oxford Characters.
A series of lithographed portraits by WILL ROTHENSTEIN, with text by F. YORK POWELL and others. 200 copies only, folio. £3 3s. net.

Pain (Barry).
THE TOMPKINS VERSES. Edited by BARRY PAIN, with an introduction. Crown 8vo. 3s. 6d.
[In preparation.

Pennell (Elizabeth Robins).
THE FEASTS OF AUTOLYCUS: THE DIARY OF A GREEDY WOMAN. Fcap. 8vo. 3s. 6d. net.

Peters (Wm. Theodore).
POSIES OUT OF RINGS. Sq. 16mo. 2s. 6d. net.

Phillips (Stephen)
POEMS. With which is incorporated "CHRIST IN HADES." Crown 8vo. 4s. 6d. net.
[Fourth Edition.

Pinkerton (T. A.).
SUN BEETLES. Crown 8vo. 3s. 6d.
[Shortly.

Plarr (Victor).
IN THE DORIAN MOOD: Poems. Crown 8vo. 5s. net.

Posters in Miniature: over 250 reproductions of French, English and American Posters with Introduction by EDWARD PENFIELD. Large crown 8vo. 5s. net.

Price (A. T. G.).
SIMPLICITY. Sq. 16mo. 2s. net.

Radford (Dollie).
SONGS AND OTHER VERSES. Fcap. 8vo. 4s. 6d. net.

Risley (R. V.).
THE SENTIMENTAL VIKINGS. Post 8vo. 2s. 6d. net.

Rhys (Ernest).
A LONDON ROSE AND OTHER RHYMES. Crown 8vo. 5s. net

Robertson (John M.).
NEW ESSAYS TOWARDS A CRITICAL METHOD. Crown 8vo. 6s. net.

Russell (T. Baron).
A GUARDIAN OF THE POOR. Crown 8vo. 3s. 6d.   [*Shortly.*

St. Cyres (Lord).
THE LITTLE FLOWERS OF ST. FRANCIS: A new rendering into English of the Fioretti di San Francesco. Crown 8vo. 5s. net.   [*In preparation.*

Seaman (Owen).
THE BATTLE OF THE BAYS. Fcap. 8vo. 3s. 6d. net. [*Fourth Edition.*
HORACE AT CAMBRIDGE. Crown 8vo. 3s. 6d. net.

Sedgwick (Jane Minot).
SONGS FROM THE GREEK. Fcap. 8vo. 3s. 6d. net.

Setoun (Gabriel).
THE CHILD WORLD: Poems. With over 200 Illustrations by CHARLES ROBINSON. Crown 8vo, gilt edges or uncut. 6s.

Sharp (Evelyn).
WYMPS: Fairy Tales. With 8 Coloured Illustrations by Mrs. PERCY DEARMER. Small 4to, decorated cover. 6s.   [*Second Edition.*
AT THE RELTON ARMS. Crown 8vo. 3s. 6d. net.
THE MAKING OF A PRIG. Crown 8vo. 6s.
ALL THE WAY TO FAIRY LAND. With 8 Coloured Illustrations by Mrs. PERCY DEARMER. Small 4to, decorated cover. 6s.   [*Second Edition.*

Shiel (M. P.).
PRINCE ZALESKI. Crown 8vo. 3s. 6d. net.
SHAPES IN THE FIRE. Crown 8vo. 3s. 6d. net.

Shore (Louisa).
POEMS. With an appreciation by FREDERIC HARRISON and a Portrait. Fcap. 8vo. 5s. net.

Shorter (Mrs. Clement) (Dora Sigerson).
THE FAIRY CHANGELING, AND OTHER POEMS. Crown 8vo. 3s. 6d. net.

Smith (John).
PLATONIC AFFECTIONS. Crown 8vo. 3s. 6d. net.

Stacpoole (H. de Vere).
PIERROT. Sq. 16mo. 2s. net.
DEATH, THE KNIGHT, AND THE LADY. Crown 8vo. 3s. 6d.

Stevenson (Robert Louis).
PRINCE OTTO. A Rendering in French by EGERTON CASTLE. Crown 8vo. 7s. 6d. net.
A CHILD'S GARDEN OF VERSES. With over 150 Illustrations by CHARLES ROBINSON. Crown 8vo. 5s. net.   [*Fourth Edition.*

Stimson (F. J.)
KING NOANETT. A Romance of Devonshire Settlers in New England. With 12 Illustrations by HENRY SANDHAM. Crown 8vo. 6s.

Stoddart (Thos. Tod).
THE DEATH WAKE. With an Introduction by ANDREW LANG. Fcap. 8vo. 5s. net.

Street (G. S.).
EPISODES. Post 8vo. 3s. net.
MINIATURES AND MOODS. Fcap. 8vo. 3s. net.
QUALES EGO: A FEW REMARKS, IN PARTICULAR AND AT LARGE. Fcap. 8vo. 3s. 6d. net.
THE AUTOBIOGRAPHY OF A BOY. Fcap. 8vo. 3s. 6d. net.   [*Sixth Edition.*
THE WISE AND THE WAYWARD. Crown 8vo. 6s.
NOTES OF A STRUGGLING GENIUS. Sq. 16mo, wrapper. 1s. net.

Sudermann (H.).
REGINA: OR, THE SINS OF THE FATHERS. A Translation of DER KATZENSTEG. By BEATRICE MARSHALL. Crown 8vo. 6s.

Swettenham (Sir F. A.)
MALAY SKETCHES. Crown 8vo. 6s.   [*Second Edition.*
UNADDRESSED LETTERS. Crown 8vo. 6s.

Syrett (Netta).
NOBODY'S FAULT. Crown 8vo. 3s. 6d. net.   [*Second Edition.*
THE TREE OF LIFE. Crown 8vo. 6s.   [*Second Edition.*

Tabb (John B.).
POEMS. Sq. 32mo. 4s. 6d. net.
LYRICS. Sq. 32mo. 4s. 6d. net.

Taylor (Una),
NETS FOR THE WIND. Crown 8vo. 3s. 6d. net.

Tennyson (Frederick).

POEMS OF THE DAY AND YEAR. Crown 8vo. 5s. net.

Thimm (Carl A.).

A COMPLETE BIBLIOGRAPHY OF FENCING AND DUELLING, AS PRACTISED BY ALL EUROPEAN NATIONS FROM THE MIDDLE AGES TO THE PRESENT DAY. With a Classified Index, arranged Chronologically according to Languages. Illustrated with numerous Portraits of Ancient and Modern Masters of the Art. Title-pages and Frontispieces of some of the earliest works. Portrait of the Author by WILSON STEER. 4to. 21s. net.

Thompson (Francis)

POEMS. With Frontispiece by LAURENCE HOUSMAN. Pott 4to. 5s. net. [*Fourth Edition.*

SISTER-SONGS: An Offering to Two Sisters. With Frontispiece by LAURENCE HOUSMAN. Pott 4to. 5s. net.

Thoreau (Henry David).

POEMS OF NATURE. Selected and edited by HENRY S. SALT and FRANK B. SANBORN. Fcap. 8vo. 4s. 6d. net.

Traill (H. D.).

THE BARBAROUS BRITISHERS: A Tip-top Novel. Crown 8vo, wrapper. 1s. net.

FROM CAIRO TO THE SOUDAN FRONTIER. Crown 8vo. 5s. net.

Tynan Hinkson (Katharine).

CUCKOO SONGS. Fcap. 8vo. 5s. net.

MIRACLE PLAYS. OUR LORD'S COMING AND CHILDHOOD. With 6 Illustrations by PATTEN WILSON. Fcap. 8vo. 4s. 6d. net.

Wells (H. G.)

SELECT CONVERSATIONS WITH AN UNCLE, NOW EXTINCT. Fcap. 8vo. 3s. 6d. net.

Walton and Cotton.

THE COMPLEAT ANGLER. Edited by RICHARD LE GALLIENNE. With over 250 Illustrations by EDMUND H. NEW. Fcap. 4to, decorated cover. 15s. net.
Also to be had in thirteen 1s. parts.

Warden (Gertrude).

THE SENTIMENTAL SEX. Crown 8vo. 3s. 6d. net.

Watson (H. B. Marriott).

AT THE FIRST CORNER AND OTHER STORIES. Crown 8vo. 3s. 6d. net.

GALLOPING DICK. Crown 8vo. 6s.

THE HEART OF MIRANDA. Crown 8vo. 5s. [*Shortly.*

Watson (Rosamund Marriott).

VESPERTILIA AND OTHER POEMS. Fcap. 8vo. 4s. 6d. net.

A SUMMER NIGHT AND OTHER POEMS. New Edition. Fcap. 8vo. 3s. net.

Watson (William).

THE FATHER OF THE FOREST AND OTHER POEMS. With New Photogravure Portrait of the Author. Fcap. 8vo. 3s. 6d. net.
[*Fifth Thousand.*

ODES AND OTHER POEMS. Fcap. 8vo. 4s. 6d. net.
[*Fifth Edition,*

THE ELOPING ANGELS: A Caprice. Square 16mo. 3s. 6d. net.
[*Second Edition.*

EXCURSIONS IN CRITICISM; being some Prose Recreations of a Rhymer. Crown 8vo. 5s. net.
[*Second Edition.*

THE PRINCE'S QUEST AND OTHER POEMS. Fcap. 8vo. 4s. 6d. net.
[*Third Edition.*

THE PURPLE EAST: A Series of Sonnets on England's Desertion of Armenia. With a Frontispiece after G. F. WATTS, R.A. Fcap. 8vo, wrappers. 1s. net.
[*Third Edition.*

THE YEAR OF SHAME. With an Introduction by the BISHOP OF HEREFORD. Fcap. 8vo. 2s. 6d. net.
[*Second Edition.*

Watson (William)—*cont.*
THE HOPE OF THE WORLD, AND OTHER POEMS. Fcap. 8vo. 3s. 6d. net.   [*Third Edition.*

Watt (Francis).
THE LAW'S LUMBER ROOM. Fcap. 8vo. 3s. 6d. net.
          [*Second Edition.*
THE LAW'S LUMBER ROOM. Second Series. Fcap. 8vo. 4s. 6d. net.
          [*Shortly.*

Watts-Dunton (Theodore).
JUBILEE GREETING AT SPITHEAD TO THE MEN OF GREATER BRITAIN. Crown 8vo. 1s. net.
THE COMING OF LOVE AND OTHER POEMS. Crown 8vo. 5s. net.
          [*Second Edition.*

Wenzell (A. B.)
IN VANITY FAIR. 70 Drawings. Oblong folio. 20s.

Wharton (H. T.)
SAPPHO. Memoir, Text, Selected Renderings, and a *Literal* Translation by HENRY THORNTON WHARTON. With 3 Illustrations in Photogravure, and a Cover designed by AUBREY BEARDSLEY. With a Memoir of Mr. Wharton. Fcap. 8vo. 6s. net.
          [*Fourth Edition.*

Wotton (Mabel E.).
DAY BOOKS. Crown 8vo. 3s. 6d. net.

Xenopoulos (Gregory).
THE STEPMOTHER: A TALE OF MODERN ATHENS. Translated by MRS. EDMONDS. Crown 8vo. 2s. 6d. net.

Zola (Emile).
FOUR LETTERS TO FRANCE—THE DREYFUS AFFAIR. Fcap. 8vo, wrapper. 1s. net.

THE YELLOW BOOK

An Illustrated Quarterly.

Pott 4to. 5s. net.

I. April 1894, 272 pp., 15 Illustrations.   [*Out of print.*

II. July 1894, 364 pp., 23 Illustrations.

III. October 1894, 280 pp., 15 Illustrations.

IV. January 1895, 285 pp., 16 Illustrations.

V. April 1895, 317 pp., 14 Illustrations.

VI. July 1895, 335 pp., 16 Illustrations.

VII. October 1895, 320 pp., 20 Illustrations.

VIII. January 1896, 406 pp., 26 Illustrations.

IX. April 1896, 256 pp., 17 Illustrations.

X. July 1896, 340 pp., 13 Illustrations.

XI. October 1896, 342 pp., 12 Illustrations.

XII. January 1897, 350 pp., 14 Illustrations.

XIII. April 1897, 316 pp., 18 Illustrations.